POLITICALLY

SINGLE

MICHAEL LEE

CONTENTS

CHAPTER 1

TO THE LEFT TO THE LEFT

They say that there are three things that you should never discuss on a first date - exes, religion, and politics. And with good reason, politics can be a tricky subject to navigate on a first date and can be the difference between having meaningless sex with someone you swiped right on via Tinder a few hours prior, to being aggressively accused of being an annually subscribed member of the Third Reich over cocktails, and all because you favour capitalism over desperately relying on free broadband from a big government under the state of the Labour Party.

My name is George Spade, I am twenty-nine years old and living in London, and I know from first-hand experience how discussing politics over a date with someone you've practically only known for five minutes can end in complete disaster – the fact that I'm conservative and not a genderfluid communist certainly doesn't help matters either in a dating scene that is quite literally swamped with maniacal leftists who treat my political views like the equivalent of diarrhoea. Conservatives are discriminated and treated disapprovingly in almost every component of life and not just on first dates – with conservatives often finding themselves ridiculed and harassed on social media, down the pub, in the classroom, and even when it comes to looking for compatible roommates who aren't intolerant of differing political views while uncomfortably sharing a flat the size of a shoebox.

But when it comes to navigating the awkward world of dating as a conservative, well, let's just say that recounting the mortifying time in which I accidentally answered the door to the local Jehovah Witnesses while wearing nothing but my Union Jack pants that my nan had brought me for Christmas doesn't win me any brownie points in the banter department, especially with my date still reeling from the fact that they have been sitting across from someone whose political outlook greatly differs from their own.

The disdain from a date becomes even more apparent after revealing to them that I had once done something so unfathomable that it had made grown men inconsolably weep like a baby and angrily protest in the street whilst they waved illiterate homemade placards in the air. Yes, I had dramatically revealed that I was a Brexiteer and had voted to leave the European Union in the 2016 referendum. It was during that moment in the date that the other person sitting opposite me, who looked like they were about to combust into flames, made their excuses and swiftly voted themselves to leave the date – never to be seen or heard from again.

This is the situation that many conservatives like myself found themselves in when swiping optimistically for a date in a very liberalised and increasingly politically correct society that had seen political differences become the deciding factor when looking for a potential significant other. And unfortunately for me, it seemed to be those who leaned more right on the political spectrum were always the ones that ended up being blocked, dumped, ghosted, and left to rot on the pile of first date carcasses. In fact, disclosing that I was riddled with genital warts and smelt of a decaying corpse each time I ejaculated would probably be met with more enthusiasm than divulging into the fact that I was a Tory with an unabashed Thatcher obsession. And as a vehement and impassioned Conservative Party voter with a Margaret Thatcher campaign poster hanging ashamedly from my bedroom wall – that could quite possibly be the reason why I still found myself ridiculously single nearing the age of thirty.

I was born and raised in Dagenham and was the only child of my mum Dawn Spade and my dad, Edward Spade. While I didn't become actively involved with politics until I turned eighteen years old, both my mum and dad were proud Conservative Party members who would routinely remind me of how much of a milestone turning eighteen was as this was the age I could now legally vote in the UK.

Some parents see their only son turning eighteen as a historical event of a young man taking his first steps into manhood and maybe even learning how to drive or moving out of the family home, but for my Tory mum and dad, turning eighteen meant that I was now officially a fully-grown Conservative Party voter and could canvas with them amid a hellacious local and national election, as the heroic Tory's fought valiantly against the villainous Labour Party on the battleground that was the polling station amongst the carnage of intensely snapped pencils and stained ballot papers. But even without my family's political influence, it was clear from a young age that I embodied the Conservative Party values of tradition, individualism, and hard work.

My first signs of conservativism began when I was three-years-old while blissfully engrossed in fiddling with a weird little dangly thing in-between my legs. That weird little dangly thing I would later go on to learn was in fact, my willy, but because my parents were so irresponsible of their parental duties, they had ignorantly just assumed my gender based on their bigoted and narrow-minded preconception of the genitalia poking out between my legs. But as a restless little baby, smashing the social and gender patriarchy was neither a concern nor on my mind, as my fidgety little hands became curiously fascinated with the little droopy thing in-between my legs.

But while that little droopy thing in-between my legs would later go on to be the sole reason why I would be hysterically accused of having 'toxic masculinity' from enraged feminists who saw me having a penis as the equivalent of possessing a weapon of mass destruction, as an easily distracted rug rat who quite clearly had very fidgety hands, I became entranced by another intimate object that didn't so happen to be my weenie, and that object was the TV.

My mum had left the front room briefly to check on the beef stew and dumplings that were cooking in the kitchen, so, left to my own devices and now seemingly bored with my little winkle, I proceeded to steadily crawl towards the TV on the 1970s abstract carpet seemingly hypnotised by the sound of a woman talking on the screen who grew louder as I crawled closer. As I reached the bottom of the wooden table that the TV was placed on, I was able to grab the edge of the panel and lift myself – now directly facing the screen as I stood on my little toes.

As I looked up, I was intensely magnetised by the static image of a stern-looking yet charismatically persuasive woman on the TV screen, wearing a royal blue skirt and jacket with sparkling white pearls elegantly draped around her neck. Her voice sounded steely and compelling, and even at three-years-old, I knew that this was a woman of authority and command. My mum walked back into the front room as I placed my lips on the TV screen as if trying to reach out to the woman talking on the screen while attempting to give her an endearing big sloppy kiss, my first instance of unsolicited sexist male chauvinism.

The woman who I was infatuated with as a baby was, in fact, former Prime Minister Margaret Thatcher – the gusty woman who would eventually be plastered on my bedroom wall as an awestruck teenager. This was also a woman who in the early nineties had been underhandly outed from her party and evicted from Downing Street after being in number 10 throughout the entirety of my childhood, with her eventual replacement John Major not exactly giving me the same kind of feels in my diaper that Thatcher had given me.

Petrified that I was about to pull the TV over and have it come crashing down over my head in a health and safety catastrophe, my mum promptly raced over and picked me up – angrily scolding me in the process and proceeding to strap me back into the confines of my highchair, where I hysterically cried down the house. While unintentionally experiencing my first dose of enforced communist authoritarian dictatorship as I desperately tried in vain to escape the confines of my prisonous highchair – a seed had been firmly planted into my tiny brain.

I became fascinated with the woman who was dubbed 'The Iron Lady' by the Soviet Union as 'Thatcherism' became the essential survival guidebook to how I lived my life. Thatcherism taught me throughout my adolescence and into adulthood that capping welfare, growing the economy, and reducing crime were great aspirations to strive for in a society, as opposed to recklessly handing out free things left right and centre while expecting the government to have all the answers for everything.

My family continued to work hard and were eventually able to buy their council house under Thatcher's 'Right to Buy' act and build a solid foundation for the Spade family to continue to prosper and to grow – now under the structure of their own privately owned roof. My dad was a grafter and was a budding entrepreneur at the age of seventeen, going on to do numerous jobs where he would end up flipping burgers, sweeping up hair in the local barbers, and handwashing cars, before finally saving enough money to pursue and start his own business. Thirty years later, and my dad is now a proud business owner of a successful minicab business, employing up to sixty drivers in the local area, and is a true embodiment of the Thatcheristic principles of working an honest day for an honest pay, living within your means, and paying your bills on time. But the Iron Lady wasn't the only strong woman in my life, as my mum was also a shining beacon of inspiration growing up in East London. My mum gave birth to me soon after she turned twenty-five and decided to become a stay at home mum, something which would infuriate so-called 'empowered' feminists of today – sending them into a deep state of prolonged unconsciousness over the absurdity that a young woman would want to become a mother and a wife and not end up a roly-poly spinster smelling of cat urine.

I remember my mum weeping uncontrollably when I moved out of the house once I turned twenty-four – from angrily shouting at me for making out with a static Margaret Thatcher, to now waving me off with tears in her eyes as I ventured off into the big wide world of responsibility driving by the determination of Thatcherism. And this is where I find myself today, as I pay an atrocious amount of money to top up my Oyster card while embarking on the long and monotonous journey into the city perched on a train that never seems to arrive on time.

While not living claustrophobically in a cupboard like most twenty-somethings who first make the move to live in the big city of London, I also managed to find a house share with housemates who didn't maliciously urinate in my tea after finding out that I was a Brexiteer - even if my vote had unintentionally affected them in the process. I was renting a small room in a four-bedroom house with three European nationals, consisting of one Pole and two Spaniards. Our picture-perfect flat was located in the colossal multicultural surroundings of Hackney in North London, and while trying my best not to be another stabbing statistic or have sulfuric acid tossed in my face from the local gangs of youth who routinely convened outside the Chicken Cottage next to our flat, I worked tirelessly and stupidly underpaid as a Marketing Assistant for a top marketing agency.

But despite the fancy job title and access to a fridge full of beer and avocados in the staff canteen, I was still just another insignificant millennial just trying to desperately cross the road without being hit by a pretentious vegan spandex-wearing cyclist, as I spent my working day constructively trying to think of calculating ways in which I could trip up bike riding hipsters who rode through red lights while making it look like an accident.

Living in London had its good and bad points, but after years of travelling on the sweltering confines of the Northern Line in the thick of the morning rush hour, I had been left with crippling depression and a disdain for humanity.

Living in Hackney certainly didn't help me with my mental health either, especially as according to national statistics it ranked as one of the most miserable areas in Britain – not surprising at all considering that Diane Abbott was also the local MP. But if having the mathematical genius that was the former bumbling Shadow Home Secretary overseeing the so-called 'People's Republic of Hackney' as our communist overlord supreme wasn't enough to give anyone suicidal tendencies, I also had a slight problem which meant that my political views and sexuality did not appropriately align together.

You see, despite living in a so-called diverse city, there was one thing that progressives and leftists could not quite come to terms with, and that was a conservative who also just so happened to be a homosexual. I found myself in the rather inconvenient position of being conservative and gay, something which was seemingly at odds with those who courageously tweeted about love and togetherness until they found out that I was a Tory. Being a gay conservative made me the equivalent of the coronavirus when it came to the LGBT community, an acronym for 'Lesbian, Gay, Bi-sexual and Transsexual' and in recent years, a radical culture and monolithic social movement and the imposed voice of those who found themselves under the rainbow arched acronym necessitated by a radical leftist culture that had methodically rounded up and grouped together a mismatch of varying sexualities, sprinkled with a little bit of gender dysphoria and trans fetishism and labelled it 'diversity'.

Pigeonholing an entire portion of society based purely on nothing more than sexual characteristics and gender identity was especially practical for those on the political left who used this type of group thinking to impose a forced narrative that gay men and lesbian women, along with bisexual and transsexual people were 'oppressed minorities' who shared the same social struggles and liberalised political ideologies. Nonconforming comrades and endangered species who would never be considered equal as long as the villainous white heterosexual man was in power and the perfect opportunity to use this scare mongering of fabricated oppression as a way to garner votes and support in national debates and elections.

Being a victim and parading the apparent 'struggle' had become a bit of a social statement in recent years, with women, ethnic minorities, and the LGBT community alike battling it out tooth and nail in the oppression Olympics. A frenzied and fraught showdown of completing marginalised and intersectional groups to determine who was the worst off, and ultimately the most oppressed. However, what made this situation even more complexing was the fact that all of the competing minority groups intensely despised one another, which was a logistics nightmare for those on the left who had exhibited multiculturalism as utopian harmony. Muslims hated the gays and didn't want LGBT propaganda forced down their ingenuous sharia children's throats. Transsexuals hated feminists and were enraged that biological women wouldn't lend them a spare tampon in the ladies' room. Illegal immigrants hated women and wanted the entire western female population barefoot and pregnant in the kitchen while making halal cupcakes in a burqa. And the LGBT community pretty much hated anyone who didn't agree with child castration and censorship.

Everyone wanted to be a perpetual victim and bask in the glorification of commercialised victimhood, but unless you were either gay, black, trans, or a non-binary amputee migrant with blue hair and a sexual fetish for antique furniture, then you couldn't quite label yourself as an oppressed minority and reap the adulation of victimhood and its social benefits.

However, if you managed to tick any of the aforementioned boxes but held traditionally conservative views – well, you could kiss that sweet victimhood and excessive admiration goodbye. Black conservatives who didn't partake in mass looting sprees, women who weren't bra-burning feminists, and even transsexuals who didn't angrily erupt in testosterone-induced rage after being unintentionally misgendered ultimately found themselves isolated by their own political and social tribes.

I found myself in the predicament of not labelling myself as a victim or even caring about my sexuality for that matter, even though my 'gay card' could undoubtfully trump the 'black' or 'female' card in the clash of oppression, as I resorted to the fact that I would never be able to reach the oppressed heights of a Syrian, transsexual with a lisping speech impediment who self-identified as an overly obese black Muslim woman every Wednesday. While the desperation to be seen as the most oppressed minority carried on, another side effect of being a compulsory victim was the assumption that being homosexual meant that I somehow automatically held left-wing views.

If an individual could tick the minority box on a diversity form, then at some point during the diversity auditing process, they would have been politically identified and assumed to be a liberal. This was called identity politics, and the political left had a stranglehold over this form of political identification and monolithic group thinking, including any chance I ever had of getting a boyfriend, or at the very least, successfully getting laid without being accused of having some kind of 'internal hatred' towards myself because I believed that being homosexual didn't define my political identity and who I voted for. Unbeknownst to me, being 'born this way' as a homosexual also meant that I was instinctually signed up without consent as a fully registered and devoted member of the LGBT community, and as a result, had to abide by the rainbow rhetoric that all lesbians, gays, bisexuals and transsexuals were required to swear unequivocal blind alliance to the righteous LGBT code of conduct and internally conditioned to think, act and vote alike.

With the LGBT acronym branded into my skin like I was multi-coloured livestock, I lost count over the number of times that people had assumed my political tendencies based on the fact that I just so happened to be a man who sucked penis.

I often found that the cult mentality of the LGBT community transcended not only over into my notifications on Twitter, where I was often angrily accused of having 'unconscious homophobia' for not willingly supporting gay sex indoctrination in nursery schools, but also having my day to day interactions with everyday people negatively impacted, with many seemingly brainwashed and engrained to think that all homosexuals were overly sensitive victims. LGBT propaganda even managed to ruin my appetite during my lunch break, as the middle-aged lady behind the till in

Marks & Spencer proceeded to casually recommend a multi-coloured 'LGBT Sandwich' stuffed with lettuce, guacamole, bacon, and tomato for me to digest, and all because she had assessed in her limited wisdom that I was gay and therefore would love the taste of conveniently coloured vegetables in my mouth.

I politely declined and instead settled for a non-political ham sandwich, as I left the store with the shame of having my sexuality commercialised and exploited by big corporations and dehumanised into rainbow-branded merchandise and patronising stereotypes. The rapid influx of LGBT boosterism and propaganda which was quite literally everywhere I went, from down the isles on supermarket shelves to inside the classroom being taught to impressionable children, was also likely the reason that acceptance of homosexuality was facing a sharp decline in the UK for the first time since the AIDS crisis of the 1980s. This, of course, didn't bode well for my public safety, especially when everyone assumed that I was associated with such degenerate people based solely on the fact that I had the same sexual preference as those who wanted to 'smash heteronormativity'. But if being gay and having the affiliation of the LGBT community attached to me like an unwanted tumour was bad enough, being homosexual while inexplicably being conservative didn't exactly do me any favours in the relationship department either.

Being gay, conservative, and single while attempting to date in London, a city that was predominantly filled with Labour Party voters and avocado eating champagne socialists was not the most ideal place to find a potential significant other, especially when everyone within proximity triggered themselves into a frenzy over my political views. Usually, when it comes to dating, normal deal-breakers in looking for the perfect match would include such deciding factors as, 'Does your date smoke?' 'Do they have a job?' and 'Are they potentially some kind of unhinged lunatic who could murder me in my sleep?' Unfortunately, in these polarising times of political differences and dissension, the line between an opposing view and a psychopath with a screw loose was becoming more difficult to differentiate between. And the more I went on dates, the more I was discovering that being conservative made people absolutely cuckoo.

My dating life had gotten so bad that Brexit probably had gone through more dates than me since the UK voted to leave the European Union, which certainty left my dating life 'dead in a ditch' as I desperately tried to complete with a referendum that had seen more manhandling than me in recent years. And while the only type of negotiation I ever engaged in these days involved my hand and my Pornhub account, being conservative meant that the only notches that were being carved into my bedpost were the days left until the Brexit transitional period was complete.

According to the political left, being gay made me one of them, and as a result of having the burden of homosexuality placed upon me, I would be forced to vote for the Labour Party while resorting to cannibalism under socialism for the rest of my life. While undergoing conversion therapy to wipe away the lingering traces of my homosexuality would certainly be an option to consider if it meant that my sexuality determined my political stance, the fact of the matter was that any logical thinking and rational person would agree that a person's sexuality did not define their political or social stance – just as the colour of a person's skin or a person's gender did not regulate what kind of views they can or cannot hold. If being gay was something in which some people were simply just born as then that person's political status shouldn't be intertwined with their sexual origination.

Regrettably, for me, I was socially shackled by the pink and fluffy chains of the LGBT community, who were frantically adding more and more letters to the LGBT acronym in their bid to be more inclusive and to garner more social authority, and, as a result, I was paraded like an identity politics exhibit alongside a miscellaneous line-up of weird and peculiar kinks, including men who thought they were women, sexualised cosplayers, and a multiverse of parallel genders that had nothing to do with my sexual orientation what so ever.

Another 'marginalised group' who were eager to put their application forward to be added to the LGBT expansion plan were paedophiles, who were now labelling adults who had an abnormal sexual attraction towards babies and pre-pubescent children as MAPS, an acronym for 'minor-attracted persons'. Because of course, in this intensely politically correct landscape of preferred pronouns and cancel culture, calling adult men and women who sexually abused young children as the universally accepted term of paedophile was apparently 'offensive' and hurt their feelings, and of course, the last thing that you would want to do is offend your friendly neighbourhood child sex offender, especially if they were a paid member of the militant LGBT community.

But if being associated with paedophilia wasn't bad enough, LGBT identity politics and the ever-growing LGBT acronym meant that by association, I, as a homosexual male, would also share the same qualities and political persuasion as that of someone with a 'furry fetish', an LGBT subculture in which grown men dressed up as anthropomorphic animal characters while rolling around the floor intensely barking and meowing like some kind of crazed sex cult on cannabis. And while I did often enjoy visiting London Zoo in the summer, I certainly did not feel the urge to erratically jump into the gorilla cage with a distant cousin of Harambe while aggressively banging on my chest in some kind of tribalistic mating call.

Sadly, however, I probably had more of a chance of finding love with an herbivorous ape than with someone who treated my political views as the equivalent of a sexually transmitted disease.

Dating was awkward enough as it was without having to defend my admiration for Theresa May's leopard print kitten heels despite her botching Brexit. And while it was easy to find common ground with many liberals and leftists who despised 'Theresa the appeaser' as much as many Conservative Party members did, when it came to matters such as climate change, free movement of people, and open borders, well, there was certainly a little less conversation and a whole lot more offensive being taken by my progressive date sitting stern-faced across from me.

I had lost count over the number of times that I had seen the sheer look of complete disgust on the face of a date when all I had done was simply reveal that I was a capitalist who encouraged the competition of a free market which offered more personal choice. However, telling a resentful Marxist that freedom of choice and responsibility are virtues in which society should be based on while they sipped on capitalist cocktails is probably not the best scenario to inadvertently point out their hypocrisy.

One guy who I thought I was on a pretty good first date with up until that point looked like he was about to evaporate into a million little pieces after I had casually mentioned in our conversation that 'transwomen' who had surgically transitioned from male to female were still biological male, even though this was scientifically true.

My date, who had been so brainwashed by the damaging effects of LGBT telepathy sincerely believed that men who underwent sex reassignment surgery could miraculously have periods, as I looked on in bafflement at the stupidity and ignorance over what I had just heard. As the seemingly controversial conversation continued, my dumfounded date made his excuses and abruptly ended the date before storming off in an effeminate hissy fit. Later that night, I found myself blocked and disregarded like the unwanted politically cadaver that I was, and all because I expressed the view that biological men who surgically removed their testicles suddenly couldn't magically grow ovaries overnight.

Unfortunately, as I had found out on more than a few occasions, for those homosexual men who did not conform to the expectation and assumption that being gay simply meant twerking, limp wrists, and a Drag Race obsession, the choice of men who did not conform to those stereotypes and who were not screaming queens or so far in the closet that they could be sharing a coat hanger with Louis Walsh was practically next to none. For as long as I continued to live in leftist London, I resigned myself to the fact that my political and social views would unreservedly cockblock me for the rest of my adult life.

CHAPTER 2

POLE TAX

It was another Monday morning in the city and I had valiantly survived another rush hour on the suffocating confines of the London Underground in which I narrowly avoided the lingering stench of coffee breath from bleary-eyed commuters while managing to walk out of the station relatively unscathed, as I made my way to another soul-destroying shift at work.

Working in the marketing industry in London guaranteed two things, I would forever be doomed to be surrounded by liberal and self-important effeminate queers with pretentious bristling beards whose utopian vision of a socialist state involved reciting the communist manifesto while sipping on oat-milk lattes.

While the other certainty of finding myself in a work environment where declaring one's preferred pronouns was as mandatory as a beer fridge and a ping pong table was the realisation that I was well and truly an outcast.

My work colleagues were toffee-nosed leftists so excessively conceited and absorbed in their own 'wokeness' that even holding the lift door open for a female co-worker was considered an 'institutionalized misogynist microaggression' which meant that I kept my distance and sat by myself during lunch. But while I had no friends at work, and any obligatory contact with colleagues was kept to an absolute minimum for fear of causing offensive and triggering a disciplinary meeting, I did have a friend who did not instantaneously break out in hives upon coming into contact with traditionally conservative views.

One of the benefits of sharing a flat with a native Pole was the fact that they were just as culturally conservative as me, if not more. Lena was four years younger than me, and at the age of twenty-five had made her way from her home city of Torun in northern-central Poland which had a population of just over 200,000 and made the move to live and work in the bright lights of London where the population exceed over eight million and with no room to swing a cat.

I first bumped into Lena in the shared kitchen of our flat whilst I found myself hastily microwaving a packet of macaroni and cheese before it expired. At first, I think that she may have been taken aback by the sight of a pale and scrawny-looking guy decked in blue and white stripy pyjamas severely blowing over a bowl of microwave food in an attempt to try and cool it down, as she judgingly leered at me from across the other side of the room with that distinctive Polish gaze of disapproval – while I looked like I was suffering from some kind of spasm attack while ferociously blowing over my bowl. However, after we had established that I was in no need of mouth to mouth resuscitation, we soon bonded over our shared love of Euroscepticism, which was ironic given that she was in the UK thanks to the free movement of people that allowed EU nationals to travel freely to live and work between other European Union countries without a visa or vetting. "Of course, I took advantage of the free movement of people, it's available, so why not use the option to travel to London and live and work here?" Lena acknowledged as I tucked into my bowl of macaroni and cheese which had since gone cold thanks to my over excessive blowing. "But I can also see why a lot of British people wouldn't like it, and I respect their decision to vote to leave the EU," Lena added, while also cementing herself in a special place in my Eurosceptic heart.

The Polish community were known for their hard work ethic, and Lena certainly embodied those qualities. "I came to the UK to start a better life for myself, but to also work hard and contribute to the country," Lena concluded, as my stomach awkwardly growled and disturbed the heart-warming patriotism that was seemingly occurring in the middle of our kitchen.

Funnily enough, I always had a fondness for Polish people as I greatly admired their patriotism and traditionalism, which had been sneered at in recent years by other European countries. I had been to the cities of Warsaw and Kraków during my trips around Europe when I first turned twenty and was amazed to see not a smudge of litter or excrement insight, let alone hear the terrorising cries of "Allahu Akbar" in the far distance before finding myself paralysed under a speeding lorry.

Poland was a country in which walking down the street didn't require a stab-proof vest or in which concrete barriers was seen as the new normal, and with good reason, the conservative government of Poland had strong anti-migrant policies and were renowned for being protective of their culture and roman catholic traditions, especially in defiance against the rise of Islamic terrorism and turbulent mass migration favoured by the European Union, which had severely crippled parts of Europe in recent years. "Poland is ranked as one of the safest countries in the world," Lena remarked, as I avidly nodded my head in agreement. Indeed, the hallowed grounds of Poland were a far cry from other European countries like Germany, Paris, and Sweden, all of whom had seen cobbled streets and picturesque towns completely turn upside down and deteriorate into intimidating 'no go zones' overnight, with local government officials desperately struggling with the tumultuous flow of young male African, Afghanistan, and Syrian immigrants arriving in droves into their communities.

Resembling more of a frenzied zombie apocalypse than an international humanitarian emergency, hysterical chaos ensured when Chancellor of Germany Angela Merkel abruptly opened the borders of Europe to an uncontrollable wave of one million immigrants in 2015, resulting in a mass inundation of unprecedented levels of crime, rape, and murder. "Immigration isn't faring that well over here either," I interjected, reflecting on the huge scale of immigration that had been initiated by then Prime Minister Tony Blair and his New Labour revolution which had resulted in over three million foreign-born people added to the population of the country since the 1997 general election. But while mass immigration was a problem in the UK, most Brits didn't hate people who were not British coming into the country as the narrative mislead the public to believe; on the contrary, they welcomed people into the country like Lena who worked hard and paid their way and who contributed to society.

However, they did have a genuine concern with the amount of people coming into the country, and the type of undesirable and often criminal characters that were being allowed to come through our borders unvetted, often ending up loitering in the streets and unashamedly calming benefits and free housing courtesy of the reluctant British taxpayers, who themselves were struggling financially without having to pay for the healthcare for gluttonous immigrants who seemingly expected freebies from a generous nation as opposed to working to pay it back. Over the years, that worry grew, as many people became troubled about how the abundance of immigration was leading to rapid cultural change, with some communities in the UK completely transformed overnight as more people with vastly contrasting cultures and traditions moved in. With public concern and uneasiness over large-scale immigration at the forefront of British politics, communal apprehension was reflected in votes, which contributed to Labour's electoral defeat in both the 2010 and 2015 general elections, and significantly aided the Brexit referendum result, as well as seeing Prime Minster Boris Johnson (who had campaigned in favour of a points-based migration vetting system) winning an overwhelming majority in the 2019 general elections and crushing the opposition in the biggest victory for the Conservative Party since Margaret Thatcher.

Meeting the unrelenting Lena, who herself had strong views against uncontrolled immigration coming from a country like Poland who always prioritised its citizens first, made a nice change from the usual suspects I glumly walked past around Hackney and the surrounding area of Islington, which always mostly consisted of white, middle class breast feeding mums shrilling about 'cultural enrichment' while probably never having seen an immigrant skulking outside their local yoga parenting class before. I and Lena would often stay up until the early hours of the morning whilst our other flatmates slept, as we put the worlds to right while lambasting the double standards of white liberal elites who treated adopting a ravenous African baby as if they were purchasing a fashion accessory that they could swagger and virtue signal around on Instagram. As myself and Lena became more acquainted, she started to open herself up about her life in Poland and the journey that brought her to the UK.

Lena had learnt English in Primary School from a young age and spoke better English than the many native English speakers who could normally be found loitering outside betting shops while reeking of weed and displaying the kind of heathen decorum that would be frowned upon in more civilised circles. Unfortunately, during her time traipsing the suburbs of London, Lena had picked up some woeful habits, particularly in using the word "Mate" in every sentence, which made her sound more like a cockney from the Eastend than a Polish girl from the small city of Torun. "Mate, can you hurry the fuck up!" Lena would berate, as I spent an eternity locked in the bathroom while intensely trying to style my hair. "Five more minutes," I would yell from the other side of the door, as I heard the faint murmurings of Lena unfavourably growling in the background.

Despite Lena sounding more like a white van man with each passing day that she spent in the UK, I greatly admired her raw candidness, and despite being brutally honest in her forthrightness, she did on occasion throw out the odd compliment. Like the time in which she made the statement that the way I spoke reminded her of the received pronunciation of how the Queen addressed her subjects, which to an obsessive royalist like myself was probably the nicest thing anyone had ever said to me.

Lena was proud of her Polish heritage, and our shared love of patriotism and national pride was a trait that we both had in common. Being patriotic or showing vigorous love for one's country had become especially problematic in recent years, with those on the left particularly showing discontent towards nationalists who proudly waved their countries flag. A prime example of this was when Labour MP Emily Thornberry abruptly quit then party leader Ed Miliband's Labour's shadow cabinet after tweeting a photo of a house in Rochester which had the banner of the England flag adorned from across its entrance.

Thornberry, who quite clearly posted the photo as a way to shame the tenants of the house, which also just so happened to have a white van parked outside the premises, the tell-tale sign of any English working-class family, was seemingly trying to insinuate that working-class people who embodied patriotic pride were somehow committing a 'racist act' in displaying an England flag from outside of their own home. While the Labour Party certainly didn't take issue when a certain blue flag with 12 stars or indeed a Palestine flag were erratically waved around during its annual conference, displaying a flag embellish with the cross of St George was a sure sign to indicate that you were indeed a white supremacist.

However, just like I didn't think that being a homosexual made me downtrodden, I also didn't think that being proud of my country made me a racist. I considered myself so stereotypically English that my ability to talk at great length about the weather to practically anyone made me the perfect test subject for the most quintessential embodiment of Britishness next to Tory Leader of the House of Commons, Jacob Rees-Mogg. And although I was incredibly proud to be English, since the Brexit referendum there had often been a negative stereotype contrived by the media regarding the British, and especially towards those who had voted to leave the European Union in the 2016 referendum.

Brexiteers as we had come to be known, were often labelled as 'xenophobic' as we basked in our unwavering hatred of people from other countries – seeing foreigners as nothing more than baristas and waiters as if they were just excess livestock leftover from the British Empire made to roast our coffee beans below the minimum wage. When in reality, it was those who voted to remain in the Brexit referendum that was often the ones left blisteringly terrified over the prospect that there would be nobody left to serve them their daily dose of turmeric lattes, and in doing so, revealing the real reasons why they wanted so desperately to stay in the European Union.

As fate would have it, Lena found herself falling into the stereotype of a diligent foreign waitress working in hospitality with

Remainers breathing a sigh of relief, as she hesitantly served up raw vegetables to supercilious and conceited hipsters at an overly priced vegetarian restaurant somewhere in Shoreditch. I would often go and visit Lena in her restaurant on a weekend during her lunch break, where we would go and grab a coffee together.

"You know what, mate, I have never been to gay pride before," Lena hinted, as we sipped on our flat white espressos during her 30 minutes away from the stench of underdone cabbage. Another quality that I greatly admired about Poland was its total rejection of the racialised LGBT ideology that had spread like a rainbow coloured virus across the western world in the last decade. One of the irritating things about living in London, apart from the extortionate price for a cappuccino and the fact that you could be stabbed by a knife-wielding hoodlum at any moment, was the yearly gay pride event that transformed the capital into something that resembled the city of Sodom.

I remember the first time I attended a gay pride event while expecting to see the usual sight of flamboyant and intoxicated scraggy queers caked in glitter and dressed as clowns in fishnets and heels while screaming that they were oppressed. And while I did see this and a whole lot of other unsavoury sights, including a grown man dressed in a baby diaper being pushed around in a pushchair by someone in a leather catsuit and latex dog mask, another observation that I made amongst the warped perversion and cringeworthy sight of the Metropolitan Police force dressed in multi-coloured tutus was the vast amount of European Union flags being waved in syndication around me.

Had I died and been resurrected in a distorted alternative reality of what the United States of Europe would look like under the dictatorship of the European Union? No, this was London in 2016, a month after the UK had voted to leave the EU, and yet here I was at a gay pride event that was supposedly about promoting the visibility and acceptance of gay men and women, but instead was a rally of disgruntled gays telling people to "Go to hell!" because there were homosexual Brexiteers within proximity who had dared use their democratic vote in a national referendum that went against what queers were supposed to think.

The gay pride event, which according to the LGBT mantra was about the promotion of gays, lesbians, bisexuals, transsexuals, and their heterosexual allies coming together in a show of diversity, love, and every other progressive cliché under the sparkle of the rainbow flag had seemingly turned into a European Union alliance march, as I inadvertently found myself caught in between queers in rainbow-coloured jockstraps and chubby lesbians with blue dyed hair waving EU flags manically in the air.

This apparent show of LGBT solidarity had become a political rally, with the only thing missing at this point being a Kylie Minogue electronic dance remix of Horst-Wessel-Lied – the anthem of the Nazi Party, but with added bebop beats to accompany a radical movement that had become intolerant and fanatical and filled with fervent queers.

Fortunately, I was not an active or partaking member of the LGBT community, and the closet thing I got to ever venturing on the gay scene was drunkenly getting lost one night in Soho after mistaking a brothel for a Chinese takeaway. Lena, even though she was Polish and conservative absolutely loved the gays and begged me to go with her to that year's annual gay pride parade. I was intensely reluctant to drag myself along as the desperate sight of squawking queers erratically waving rainbow flags in my face certainly didn't feel my heart with exhilaration, let alone pride.

However, this would be Lena's first ever gay pride event that she would ever attend, as coming from Poland, the country in which LGBT was the sign of the devil and everything wrong in the world, the closest thing to seeing a gathering of promiscuous men in one place together would have been the local whore house, so the least I could do was take her along to witness a few thousand gay men ass clapping in rhythm. Lena was excited to experience her first dose of LGBT public inculcation as she rejoiced at the prospect of attending the event in London – while not wanting to be the one to deprive her of the recoiling sight of the fawning Mayor of London Sadiq Khan awkwardly sashaying with severely overweight middle-aged drag queens who looked more like cheap toilet roll covers than justifiable members of society.

So, despite my initial uneasiness and discomfort of being within proximity of a mass crowd of unhinged queers, I hesitantly agreed to accompany Lena to her first gay pride event – even if I would be compromising my mental health in the process.

CHAPTER 3

INDEPENDENCE GAY

"Fuck me, mate!" Lena gasped in shock, as we walked past the sight of two bearded muscular men in nothing but their pants gyrating to the blaring sound of Britney Spears being played over the speakers. We walked further down the street where we were then met with the sight of another scantily clad man who looked like he was long past retirement age as he danced around in the middle of the road while penetrating himself with what looked like a large rainbow coloured dildo.

I looked away in horror at the sight of an OAP fingering himself in public as a family with young children, who had taken a wrong turn, walked on by in visible distress – while shielding their kids from the monstrosity that was occurring around them. I had just introduced a young conservative Polish woman to her first glimpse of what to expect on a gay pride rally in London, and to say that she was taken aback by what was occurring around her was truly an understatement, as we continued to push past hordes of testosterone and thongs. We had just made our way out of Oxford Circus Station and up towards the Shaftesbury Memorial Fountain, where we were instantaneously blinded by the sight of rainbow flags everywhere. I found myself deep in a crowd of multicolours and pansies and was already contemplating the most effective way to commit suicide as I gripped onto Lena with dear life.

But whilst I wrestled with depression and suicidal thoughts, Lena was opening up to the idea of being surrounded by half-naked men in nothing but spandex and glitter. And being the good friend that I was, I decided to halt my melancholy and pensive sadness from dampening her fun, and so I decided to get paralytically drunk instead, so I could cope with my immoral surroundings that felt like it was closing in from around me. While having blurred vision and not being able to think coherently may not have been the best decision to make in hindsight, it certainly made being around socialist queers who were offended at absolutely everything a lot more tolerable, as I continued to swiftly guzzle down my can of cider to numb the reality that I was amid a sea of shrieking unclothed homosexuals in London gay pride.

Gay pride was born out of the events of the June 1969 Stonewall riots, which saw frenzied protests and often violent demonstrations by members of the gay community against the police of New York after a string of police raids on one of the only gay bars at the time, the Stonewall Inn. 50 years later and what was originally a singular annual event had now spawned into an entire month of gayness, as businesses and leading corporations fought over themselves in a bid to cash in on what had become a marketing publicity opportunity in LGBT inclusiveness. 'Look at us! We love and support gay people! Look! We have hideously drenched rainbow colours all over our corporate logo! We are super diverse!' was the desperate vibe that I got from the multi-coloured cash dispenser as I attempted to check my bank balance using a cashpoint that looked like it had been heaved over with rainbow spew, as I proceeded to withdraw my money from the dispenser which thankfully still only had one imprinted queen on it who wasn't a venomous effeminate queer with an attitude problem and victim complex.

In just a few decades, the LGBT community had gone from wanting equality to now wanting privilege, as the multi-coloured movement continued its indoctrination of young children with the trojan horse of gay penguins. Two cans of cider, three shots of tequila, and a whole lot of inappropriate grouping occurring around me later, and I was officially away with the fairies – literally! After the parade of kaleidoscopic gender-bending queers had packed up for the day, Lena begged me to take her to her first gay bar. While being bladdered had its drawbacks, such as the inevitable hangover that I would be nursing in the morning – I was absolutely wrecked, and so in a moment of intoxicated brash foolhardiness, I took her by the hand and walked towards the demonic netherworld that was Soho.

Soho was that sordid and often disreputable part of London where you could purchase cocaine from a prostitute on the way to the pub, and then walk down the road and get a handjob from a retired barrister in a backroom gay cinema while watching a 1970's homoerotic porno. If Soho was embroiled amid tribal postcode wars in which drug gangs carved up territory in local boroughs while attacking neighbouring rivals if they dared set foot in the wrong street, then Soho was unquestionable the property of the undisrupted gay mafia.

We strolled past the flickering neon lights of sex shops with chains and whips hanging scenically from across the window as rainbow flags flew freely in the evening sky suspended from every building along the street. "Mate, I think they have gone a bit over the top with the rainbow flags," Lena observed, as I staggered along the cobbled road of Old Compton Street with mandatory drunken haze in check.

It seemed that while homosexuality didn't particularly bother or offend Lena (unlike many of her fellow country people), like me, she questioned the homogeneous uniformity of the LGBT community, and why those who were strenuously huddled together under the acronym of gayness – were all expected to be feather boa wearing liberals. It made me feel thankful that I was fortunate enough to be a teenager when Section 28 was still in full effect. a law passed by Margaret Thatcher's Conservative Party which banned the promotion of homosexuality by local authorities in Britain's schools.

I wondered if I would have potentially ended up like the perverted pensioner with his sagging bum cheeks out in full view had I not been fortunate enough to be a teenager under Section 28. I felt relieved knowing that I did not have a pink-haired leftist teacher instil upon a young and impressionable George that sexuality was an identity and that wearing nothing but a thong and a pair of leather boots in public would be socially acceptable going into adulthood.

Fortunately, I was wearing neither a thong nor pair of leather boots, nor did I have a lunatic of a teacher brainwash me into thinking that my sexuality made me oppressed, as we continued walking through the crowd of drunken queers who were anything but a victim. While I wallowed in my scorn for identity politics, Lena was still enjoying being surrounded by so many flamboyant men. Despite her sceptical conservatism, Lena was still very much a young woman, and like many young women in a western country, she inherently loved the gays. And like most self-proclaimed 'fag hags' who gripped onto their gay best friend like they were the greatest thing since sliced organic bread, Lena probably just enjoyed the novelty of going to a nightclub and dancing with a man who didn't want to get into her knickers but instead who just wanted to borrow them for the night after she was done with them.

"George! I fucking love you, mate!" Lena screamed at the top of her lungs over the thumping beat of repetitive dance music from the '90s, as we briskly knock-backed our sixth screaming orgasm shot of the night in the appropriately named Club Climax. We were in quite possibly the gayest nightclub in Soho, and an inebriated Polish woman had just drunkenly declared her undivided love for me. "When are we going home?" I pleaded with Lena, hoping that she would hear the despair in the tone of my voice and have pity on me.

Even in a state of drunken befuddlement, I still knew that being surrounded by a cluster of shrieking queers was not good for my state of mind. "Oh, George! Just one more dance, please mate," Lena insisted, as I resorted to the fact that I was quite literally trapped in hell with nowhere to go. After dancing what felt like an entirety to tedious techno music, Lena finally wanted to have a break from spinning and twirling on the dancefloor and sit down. As we made our way to the seating area and perched comfortably in our seats, I couldn't help but notice a group of men sitting a few seats away from us. While I couldn't quite hear what they were saying over the monotonous electronic beats, I could unmistakably make out their American accents.

Huddled around the table as they consumed their drinks, all three of the men were considerably good-looking, but it was one in particular that caught my eye. The man in question had a tan-skinned complexion with dark brown eyes and brunette hair shaved on the sides with a spikey mop of hair on top. He was wearing the tightest trousers that I had quite possibly ever seen, with the tightness of the trousers showing off the rounded shape of his muscular thighs. As he laughed in mid-conversation with his two acquaintances, I caught a glimpse of his teeth through the darkened faded lights of the nightclub, and they were as white as a sparkling pearl on the shores of a windswept beach.

I was officially besotted and drunk enough to go over to the groomed group only a few seats away and make an utter tit of myself in a desperate bid to try and flirt, but thankfully, that imposing conservative voice of Margaret Thatcher miraculously appeared in the nick of time while in the middle of Club Climax and simply told me "No! No! No!" Listening to my inner Maggie and admitting defeat, I looked over to the right of me to indicate to Lena that we were categorically going to go home now – only to see her fast asleep and passed out on the sofa.

"Well, this is just great," I grumbled out loud to myself, as I firmly nudged her in a vain attempt to get her to wake up. I found myself in a bit of an awkward predicament while caught somewhere between a group of hot American men and an unconscious Pole, as I desperately tried to get Lena to wake from her sozzled slumber. I sighed out loud in frustration as I looked out to the dancefloor of whirling gay men who were now gathering in synchronised formation to perform the YMCA dance made famous by the Village People.

As I watched on in mortification, I noticed that two of the Americans had walked onto the dancefloor to join in on the shenanigans, leaving the other American with the big thighs alone by himself. As I gazed intensely at the handsome man who was now sat by himself, I suddenly received a jolt of shock as he abruptly spun his head around and made direct eye contact with me – catching me in the act of inappropriately perving in the process. I rapidly looked away with great speed as any Brit would do when caught in the act of making awkward eye contact as I proceeded to intensely look at the floor. However, before I could dissolve into the chair and wish that I had never been born, I could see the big thighed American get out of his chair from the corner of my eye and make his way towards my direction, as I took a deep breath and experienced a mild rush of panic.

"Hey there, how are you?" said a deep sounding voice, as I looked up to see the dishy man standing next to me.

"I'm great, thanks for asking, how are you?" I shyly mumbled, while attempting to hide the fact that I was pissed out of my head and amid a frenzied panic as the well-proportioned American towered over me.

He looked over at Lena who at this point was lying face down and spread out on the sofa like an exhausted hooker after a hard night's work. "And who is your friend?" he laughed while pointing to a senseless Polish woman. "Oh, that's Lena, she's currently off her tits," I joked while drunkenly laughing at my British dry wit in the process. "And what's your name?" he asked, as I tried to keep a fixed gaze into his dark brown alluring eyes without abruptly melting. "My name is George," I responded, as I began to feel the faint drips of sweat slide down from my forehead.

"And what is yours?" I asked while half expecting that he would reply with a stereotypical male American name like Chad or Connor. "I'm Ronald, pleasure to meet you, George," he smiled, as I discretely tried to rub away the sweat dripping down my forehead by making it look like I was scratching an itch instead. Ronald was sexy, masculine, and suitably had the same first name as the 40th president of the United States of America and Margaret Thatcher's BBF, Ronald Reagan.

One hour, thirteen minutes, and promptly sobered up later, and I had been having the most incredible conversation with Ronald who had now moved from his seat and was now sitting beside me. Taking into consideration that we were surrounded by booty popping queers and was sat next to an immobilized drunk Polish woman, we were having quite the exchange, an exchange that surprisingly didn't involve asking one another about our preferred sexual position in the bedroom department – considering that 90% of all initial interactions in gay clubs ultimately lead to sex in the toilet cubicles.

During our conversation, I learnt that Ronald was born in the state of Tennessee and was currently visiting London as a tourist for the first time. He was twenty-four years old and was on a gap year studying psychology and fittingly decided to visit the UK. He had arrived with his cousin Joey and his best friend Matthew, who were the two other men he was with, and on a whim ended up in Club Climax after getting free entry from a promotional boy who had flirted with them outrageously. Both Joey and Matthew were still grinding on the dancefloor, which left me perfectly alone with Ronald as we got onto the subject of his sexuality.

"So, are you gay?" I curiously asked Ronald, while wanting to address the rainbow coloured elephant in the room before making an ill-advised pass at someone who didn't even bat for my team. "No, I'm bisexual," laughed Ronald, before proceeding to wink at me while making me feel all fidgety inside. "Bisexual?" I gushed, while also acquiring the confirmation that I was looking for that my attempts at flirtation were at least not misdirected. "Yeah, that's right, and what about yourself?" he asked, as I unwieldy shuffled around in my seat. "Well, the last time I checked, I was indeed a homosexual," I sniggered, as I once again amused myself with my extraordinary level of wittiness.

It was in that moment that I began to hear the tumultuous mumblings of noise as I looked over to see that Lena had awoken from her state of wooziness, and in the process had proceeded to vomit all over the floor. "Is your friend OK?" Ronald asked, as I quickly stood up from my seat and rushed over to Lena to attempt to get her up from the sofa. "Oh, she's fine, she just can't handle her drink," I joked back, as I put Lena's arm over my shoulder and walked her towards the toilets, while also potentially leaving behind the father of my future children because of a sloshed Pole.

After making our way to the gender-neutral toilets, we found an empty cubicle inside as I closed the door behind us whilst Lena swiftly stuck her head down the toilet and proceeded to produce demonic sounds as she spewed up an entire bar worth of alcohol. Here I was, in a gay club and locked in a cubicle toilet with an apparent Polish demon who was heaving all over the place and sounding like she was being exorcised, while the man of my dreams sat calmly by himself surrounded by twinks and trannies, as I envisioned promiscuous queers circling him like bisexual prey in my absence. After what felt like ten minutes of puking up everything but the kitchen sink, Lena's head reappeared from the toilet.

"Who was that guy you were talking to?" stammered Lena, as she gingerly tried to get up from the cubicle floor. "Oh, just some guy," I coly replied, while not wanting to make a big deal over the fact that I had fallen head over heels in love with some obscure American tourist in the middle of a gay club in Soho. "Mate, I feel like shit, I'm going to get an Uber and go home," Lena revealed, as she unlocked the door to the cubicle and staggered out of the gender-neutral toilet still with smudges of sick on her t-shirt – stumbling past a queue of towering drag queens who leered over Lena with a disapproving gaze after hogging the cubicle for so long. "Are you coming with me?" Lena asked, while probably expecting that I would respond with a resounding yes, especially as I had hopelessly begged her to leave with me as soon as we stepped foot into the club a few hours prior.

"Erm... I think I'm going to stay for a bit," I sheepishly replied, as Lena looked on in confusion. "But I thought you hated being around gays?" she insisted, as I simply shrugged my shoulders. "Well... I told that guy that I would hang out with him,"

I gushed, as Lena looked at me fixedly with a suspicious stare. "Ah, I see, well, say no more," Lena insisted, as a small twinkie of a knowing smile appeared on her face.

We stopped just before the exit of the club, where a Brit and a Pole exchanged an affectionate hug that was unconventional for our conservative cultural traditions. "Are you going to be OK getting home?" I asked, as Lena took her phone out from her pocket and began to order an Uber. "I'll be fine, don't worry about me," insisted Lena, as she briskly rubbed off the remains of vomit that was smeared on her shirt. "But mate, if you are going to invite him back to the flat, make sure you fuck quietly!" Lena cautioned as she walked through the threshold of the club door.

With Lena gone and hopefully safe with an Uber driver who wasn't a member of ISIS, I made my way through the wave of effeminate gays on the dancefloor and back towards the sofa area and where I had left Ronald. Emerging from the horde of queers unscathed, I arrived at the sofa area and basked in the sight of Ronald still sitting contently by himself, as I walked towards him with a beaming smile etched on my face. "Hey, you're back," Ronald grinned, as I proceeded to sit back down onto the chair.

But as I was about to sit down beside him, I instantaneously slipped on a speck of Lena's vomit that was smeared on the floor and, in doing so, fell headfirst on Ronald – finding my face planted directly into his crotch. "Well, this is quite a compromising position," Ronald laughed, as I apologised and swiftly picked myself back up while perching awkwardly beside him. But before I even had a chance to compose myself over the embarrassing episode that had just occurred, Ronald leaned his head inwards towards mine and proceeded to place his lips on to my mouth, and before you know it, we were kissing.

I closed my eyes and placed my arms around his chiselled body, as we embraced and passionately kissed underneath the dimmed lights that were flickering between a shade of blue and a colour of red, as I placed my arms on his chest while I leisurely felt the fabric of his shirt. But then, all of a sudden, he stopped kissing me, and swiftly pulled away from me as I opened my eyes in shock. "What's wrong?" I gasped, as I looked up from the sofa to see two towering men starring back at me. "Oh, hey guys, this is George. George, meet Joey and Matthew," Ronald gushed, as I promptly perched myself up from the sofa and awkwardly shook the hands of the two men standing over us. The two men in question were the same men who I had seen Ronald talking with earlier in the night, and who had now seemingly returned from the dancefloor after throwing wincing handshapes in the air during YMCA.

"I see you've been familiarizing yourself with the locals," laughed one of the men, as I hastily sat back down on the chair beside Ronald. "This is my cousin Joey I told you about," Ronald signalled to me, as I timidly nodded my head in acknowledgement. "Hey, move up," ordered the other guy, who I assumed was Matthew, as I tried to make space for him to sit on the arm of the chair.

As Ronald began to talk to his cousin Joey beside me, Matthew leaned in towards me. "So… you and Ronald, eh?" Matthew teased, as I looked across at him with a reddened face and uncomfortable with the entire situation. "He's a cool guy, you have nothing to worry about," Matthew reassured, as I knowingly smiled.

Ronald was a nice guy; in fact, he was a great guy, and even though I was plastered when I originally met him, after almost two hours of sobering conversation and a nimble kiss, I didn't want my first meet with Ronald to be my last. It was fast approaching the early hours, and I was beginning to feel tired as I let off a raucous yawn. "Someone is tired," observed Ronald, as he gave me an acknowledged smile. "I'm feeling pretty beat too actually, maybe it's time we get out of here," Ronald suggested, as both Joey and Matthew briskly nodded their heads in agreement.

Joey and Matthew walked on ahead, as Ronald waited for me to perch myself from off the sofa. "I've had a good time tonight," smiled Ronald, as he reached out his hand and looked at me tellingly. Looking back at him, I extended my arm out and held my palm out with my fingers stretched out, and before you know it, we were both holding one another's hand.

I held his hand tightly as he led me through the flock of howling gay men who were still bopping along to the same repetitive dance music on the dancefloor. We crossed the threshold of the exit of the club and found ourselves back onto the soiled streets of Soho as a chilly breeze shivered my spine. "Are you cold?" asked Ronald, before bringing me forward towards his chest.

With his muscled arm wrapped around my shoulders and my head perched on his bicep, we walked through the empty streets of London, quietly vacant of prostitutes and posturing queers, as Joey and Matthew walked on ahead in front of us. As the sounds of wakened birds chirping in the distance signalled the arrival of daybreak, I couldn't help but wonder about the kiss that I and Ronald had shared, and if I should cherish this moment in the grip of his arms for it could be our last.

As we walked comfortably silent along Tottenham Court Road, I immediately felt a sudden urge of apprehension as we drew closer to the station. I didn't expect to find myself at a gay pride parade, let alone walking the streets of London with a muscled American who I had pulled in a gay bar, and as we walked closer to the station I knew that this night could also end the way most nights did, with myself travelling on the Northern Line alone surrounded by intoxicated boisterous chavs.

"So, what are your plans for tomorrow?" I nervously asked Ronald, as we found ourselves standing closely together outside the entrance of the tube station as weary commuters stood idly on the escalators making their way deeper underground. "Making plans to see you," beamed Ronald looking intensely into my eyes before he slowly tilted his head towards my lips and kissed me.

CHAPTER 4

MAKE AMERICA DATE AGAIN

T he last time an Englishman had fallen this hard for an American, the monocracy almost collapsed and the crown was suddenly abdicated, but unlike Wallis Simpson and Edward VIII, my American love interest only had a limited amount of time left on his tourist visa, and I was determined to get him to stay and begin his application for British citizenship immediately. I had been on two dates with Ronald, with each date making me stupidly fall for him more and more.

Our first date was at a dodgy Chinese buffet restaurant somewhere in Kings Cross, whose owner I believed had deliberately infused the sweet and sour chicken with some sort of Chinese communist delirium drug. A while after we had left the restaurant, I began to feel nauseous and started to hallucinate fire breathing dragons flying around North London, but in reality, I was probably absurdly intoxicated from the obscene amount of wine I had consumed rather than being under the influence of communist mind control whilst swearing unequivocal blind alliance to President Xi Jinping. Our second date didn't fare much better either, as I proceeded to fall face-first into a puddle as I awkwardly tried to avoid a black cab driver from committing homicide and killing me on what was supposed to be a romantic evening out in Knightsbridge. However, despite almost being black cab roadkill and paranoidly thinking that I was pledging alliance to a fascist communist government while under the influence of drugs, I loved spending time with my American lover.

Ronald, along with Matthew and Joey, were in the UK for another two weeks and we're planning to go back to America at the end of the month after spending their final week in Northern Ireland. While we had been on two official dates so far, I and Ronald had never actually discussed the future and whether or not this was going to be just a holiday fling or a long-distance relationship that would eventually lead to paying a surrogate mum from Ethiopia in having our children.

While talk of adopting third-world children was not on the table just yet, we did discuss seeing one another again as we planned our third date later on in the week. We arranged to go to a bar in Shoreditch and grab a drink before heading off to catch a film, and while the prospect of being surrounded by pretentious millennials didn't exactly feel my heart with glee – having another date with Ronald certainly did. I waited outside Old Street Station for Ronald to arrive as the stench of organic roasted coffee beans filled the air.

Shoreditch was hipster territory and was brimming with bearded millennials who drank cocktails from jam jars beneath the backdrop of anti-capitalist graffiti sprayed across every building that didn't happen to be an organic avocado pop-up café. "Hey gorgeous," I heard from a husky voice behind me, before swiftly turning around to see Ronald standing there. "Hey!" I beamed, before leaning in and greeting Ronald with a nimble hug. "You look nice today," Ronald smiled affectionately, as he held me in closer while he tenderly wrapped his arms around me. "Thanks, so do you," I giggled, as the whiff of Ronald's aftershave drifted past my inhaled nostrils. We wandered through the streets of Shoreditch, trying to find a particular bar that Ronald had read positive reviews about online. "They serve drinks in miniature kitchen sinks," Ronald excitedly twinkled, as I looked on less enthusiastically over the prospect of gulping alcohol from household appliances.

Finally, after navigating through darkened alleys and almost having another near-fatal collision with a maniacal black cab driver, we found ourselves outside the ironically named Tipsy Cow Bar. Ironic because at just over twenty quid per cocktail, there was more chance of me being a thirsty cow than a tipsy cow by the end of the night.

We made our way into the bar and, to my complete surprise, we managed to find two seats and a table in the corner that was not occupied by conceited hipsters. Considering that this was a Saturday night in Shoreditch and also during the peak hour of drunken feminists demanding equal opportunity at the bar while also expecting their emasculated boyfriend to pay for the bar tab at the end of the night – this was a pretty rare find.

After steering through the sea of moustached indie kids that had assembled above the swaying glitterball hanging from the ceiling, I managed to make my way to the bar and reluctantly part ways with forty pounds from my bank account in the process after ordering two exorbitant cocktails served in a scaled-down washing machine and microwave respectively. With both overly priced kitchen appliances firmly in hand, I made my way back to the table where Ronald was sitting and perched our washing machine and microwave cocktails down on the table. "So, I've paid forty pounds to drink alcohol from my mum's kitchen appliances," I laughed, as I attempted to take a sip from my washing machine cocktail currently whirling around with cranberry juice and vodka, as Ronald looked equally absurd drinking from a miniature microwave. Even though we had been on three dates since we first met in Soho, I had yet to broach the delicate subject of politics up to Ronald.

I had intentionally avoided the subject of politics with Ronald all together, and with good reason, as every time I had injected politics into the conversation on previous dates, I always ended up walking to the tube station alone at the end of the night after revealing that Margaret Thatcher was my life muse. But after three dates of getting to know him, I figured that Ronald was unlikely to erupt in a rage of fire and brimstone after learning that I was a conservative.

So, what better way to get onto the subject of politics than by talking about Ronald's namesake, the former American President, Ronald Regan. "So, you never told me about your name," I questioned Ronald while sipping on my extortionate miniature washing machine. "Well, my mum was a huge Ronald Regan fan, so that's basically where the name came from," Ronald laughed, as he guzzled down his rum and grapefruit cocktail currently circulating in his minuscule microwave. Jackpot! I was currently on a date with a hot American who was not only swigging cocktail from a microwave but who was also named after the former Republican U.S. President. This could quite possibly be the greatest date I had ever been on, I thought to myself, as I relished in the fact that I had potentially found my political soulmate.

"So, that would make you a Republican then?" I smiled broadly, as I firmly placed my washing machine cocktail onto the table in anticipation of his answer. "Fuck no!" erupted Ronald, as he intensely leered at me with disgust as if I had just killed a kitten and penetrated a goat. "I'm a Democrat! Fuck Trump!" Ronald continued raging, as he aggressively placed his microwave cocktail onto the table while still intensely looking at me from across the table. I had seen that look a thousand times before, and it was often a look from the widened pupils of a leftist who had just encountered a political opinion that their immune system couldn't quite accept, as they reacted with the poise and rationale of a tempered infant throwing a fit.

"Please don't tell me you are a fucking conservative?" snapped Ronald, as I looked on in distress upon being angrily asked a question that would make any conservative amid a date with an angered Democrat tremble with fear. "Erm... I... I am," I stammered, as I felt my bum checks nervously grow tense in suspense of the reaction I was about to receive. "Oh..." gasped a stunned Ronald, as he confusingly gazed at me with a look of bewilderment etched across his face.

There was a paused silence as Ronald starred intensely at the table – not making any effort to make eye contact with me as if lost in thought and trying to process the realisation that he was sitting across from a conservative on a date. "So, what makes you a conservative?" Ronald asked, now looking up at me with a perplexed expression on his face – as if he had never met someone with views that differed to his own before.

It was the same muddled look from the person sitting across from the table that I had seen many times before, as the penny finally dropped that they were on a romantic evening with someone who believed in a small government. "Well, ultimately, I believe in the responsibility of the individual and not the state." I firmly answered, as I picked my washing machine cocktail from the table and took a quick sip to wash my mouth which had become dry with nerves. "But don't you think that a government has a responsibility to take care of the vulnerable and those who are less fortunate such as refugees?" Ronald insisted, as the perfect date that I had been on just a few moments prior began to metamorphose into a screeching social justice warrior before my very eyes.

"No, I believe that individuals should take responsibility for their actions and circumstances and make the best of a situation no matter how bad it is," I maintained, as I took another slurp from my washing machine. "Allowing undocumented mass amounts of people into a country not only lowers the economy and increases the level of crime but also completely deteriorates the communities they are placed in, which always become progressively worse as a result," I added, as Ronald looked on with a frowned expression now firmly embedded on his face – which also looked to be getting progressively worse as his frown line widened as the conversation continued.

"So, you believe in borders then?" Ronald rebuked, as I began to see small wisps of silver-grey smoke intensity rise from the top of his head. Borders and the topic of refugees always hit a nerve point with leftists, as they were always unequivocally pro-open borders, but seemingly had never themselves adopted a 'defenceless and vulnerable' refugee child or visited a no-go zone in the outer suburbs of cities in which mass immigration had created a hornet's nest of crime and poverty, as I tried to figure out a way to handle this topic without inadvertently making Ronald look like a virtue-signalling hypocrite in the process.

"Well, to quote the great man who you were named after – a nation that cannot control its borders is not a nation," I remarked while trying my best not to look superiorly smug across from a stern-faced Democrat who looked like he was just about ready to explode. "Wow! What an arsehole!" sneered Ronald, as I looked on in disbelief at being belligerently dammed because I had just quoted Ronald's namesake. "I beg your pardon!" I bleated, as I promptly sat up from my chair - taken aback over what was transpiring before my eyes.

"You heard!" Ronald growled. "What an inconsiderate fucking arsehole you are!" he angrily roared, now looking at me with furiously chiselled disgust on his face as if he had accidentally just stepped into dog excrement. "What is wrong with you?" I exclaimed as I began to feel my heart intensely thump with anxiety. While I had encountered my fair share of exasperated liberals in London, never had I come across an infuriated Democrat before, especially an Americans Democrat, who was most notorious as being extremely wild and unhinged in their intolerance towards those with opposing views, as I was finding out to be scarily accurate as Ronald unleashed his full wrath from across the table.

"Don't tell me you fucking like Trump too!?" cautioned Ronald, now intensely staring at me with trembling pupils – angrily anticipating what my answer would be. Being conservative was one thing, but being a Trump supporter was another, and was seen as the ultimate sign of apparent Nazism and everything hateful in the world by a leftist.

I had two choices, I could either downplay my Trumpism and not mention the fact that I had a MAGA hat stuffed in my sock drawer, or I could be entirely honest and mention my love for the democratically elected President of the United States casually in the conversation. What was the worst that could happen, I thought to myself, as I let out a relenting "Of course!" without any hesitation. Ronald raised his eyebrows and abruptly sat back into his seat – his head perched up towards the ceiling while intensely looking up and not saying a single word but just quietly gazing up into the ceiling, as I continued rambling about my love for Trump.

"Trump has grown the American economy in his time in office, while also achieving the lowest ever African, Asian, and the

Hispanic unemployment rate in the history of the country," I remarked, as Ronald slowly lowered his head from the view of the ceiling and proceeded to make direct eye contact with me – starring back at me with the same arched eyebrows that had scrutinized me before. I knew that saying anything that was remotely favourable towards Trump in front of an American Democrat would garner a negative reaction, especially someone who was mentally unbalanced as Ronald, who was suffering from the damaging effects of Trump derangement syndrome.

I had read about the symptoms of Trump derangement syndrome on the internet but had never been this close to a real-life case study before, as Ronald began to display all of the associated signs linked with the disease. Also referred to in the medical field as 'TDS', this internalised chronic mental condition made those suffering from its devastating effects experience such intensified hatred of President Trump that it greatly impaired judgment of individuals in its grip while altering them to nothing more than clinically insane intolerant psychopaths who were intolerant of ideas of nationalism and pride.

The severe ramifications of coming down with a bad case of Trump derangement syndrome in a leftist and especially a Democrat were long-lasting – becoming easily prone to breaking out in rashes and extreme anger when faced with signs of patriotism towards America, and specifically in favour of the democratically elected President of the United States, as I was finding out myself. "So basically, I'm on a date with a fucking Nazi!" shouted Ronald, as the bearded hipsters that had been contently sipping cocktails out of lightbulbs instantaneously leered over in my direction upon hearing the 'N' word being shouted from across the bar. "A Nazi!?" I gasped in astonishment, as I looked around at the bar to notice that everyone was now gawking in my direction. Labelling someone as a Nazi because they had opposing political views was hardly new, and in recent years had often been the go-to tactic when a leftist was on the losing end of the argument – which more often than not was normally the case. But even though I had been labelled a Nazi numerous times before, being compared to the Third Reich on a date was certainly not the most pleasant of experiences, especially considering that I had liked Ronald who by now was looking at me as if I had just inappropriately yelled "Hail Hitler!" in the middle of the bar.

"He called all Mexicans fucking drug dealers and rapists!" fumed Ronald, as he aggressively thumbed the table with the palm of his hands – inadvertently knocking over my washing machine cocktail in the process. The thing that I had learnt about leftists in my dealings with them was that they were often prone to exaggerating half-truths or completely fabricating reality in their attempt to justify their warped delusion, as I proceeded to counteract Ronald's absurd claim that Trump had labelled all Mexicans as rapists.

"Trump was specifically referring to illegal immigrants and criminal gangs crossing the Mexican border," I replied, as I picked up my knocked over washing machine cocktail from off the floor. But before I had time to even place my washing machine the right way around on the table, Ronald had stormed off. "Where are you going!?" I yelled at Ronald, as he frenziedly stomped off into the distance. I hastily sprang up from off my chair and dashed towards him, as I sprinted up from behind him and gripped on to his arm.

"Are you serious!?" I bellowed, as he promptly stopped walking and turned around to face me. "Fuck off, Nazi!" he screamed, before yanking my hand off his arm and proceeding to heavily pace towards the entrance of the bar. I stood silently stunned and in disbelief over how complimenting a strong Trump economy and record-high employment figures suddenly amounted to me being an apparent Nazi and ended up with Ronald stomping off in a fit of rage, as I quickly made my way through the threshold of the bar entrance and out onto the street. As I stood on the street corner, where the bar was located, I saw Ronald from across the road angrily stomping off into the distance, as I stood on the edge of the pavement – unable to move as a line of vehicles drove across the road in front of me.

"Ronald!" I shouted from across the street as I desperately tried to get his attention. But he didn't turn around, instead, I looked on from the edge of the pavement as Ronald walked off into the distance, before disappearing entirely amongst the backdrop of towering buildings shaped like vibrators. And just like that… he was gone.

Here I was, living in the capital of one of the greatest countries in the entire world during the peak years of capitalism, democracy, and Gemma Collins memes, and I had just unceremoniously been dumped in the middle of Shoreditch, surrounded by gaping liberal arts students and forty pounds out of pocket, and all because I made a passing comment that I was a fan of the democratically elected President of the United States.

What was it about being conservative that made these supposedly tolerant leftists so infuriated and enflamed with hatred that they would react with such excessive outbursts, I pondered to myself, as I waited for the oncoming vehicles to stop before crossing the road. As I walked down the steps of Old Street Station feeling disheartened, I went around in my head over exactly what had just happened and how I had once again found myself being publicly scrutinised because of my political opinions. It made me question whether I was a bad person for wanting strong borders while reflecting on my morals and values. I knew that I was a good person, and I knew that without the core principles of conservatism and capitalism, society would deteriorate into absolute socialist chaos. I certainly never pushed my views onto people unless it was a mutual conversation, and I had never done or said anything that was not based in fact or logic, yet it seemed that I was still unintentionally triggering people while also ruining my love life in the process.

After an excruciatingly long journey home on the Northern Line, which included a group of middle-aged women on a hen night drunkenly belting out renditions of Rick Astley that sounded more like wailing cats being dismembered and decapitated than actual singing, I finally arrived back in the People's Republic of Hackney as I let myself into the house. "So, how was your date?" inquired Lena, as I walked into the front room whilst she sat with our other flatmates spread out on the sofa eating pizza and watching Britain's Got Talent on the TV. "Oh, he dumped me because I told him I was a Trump fan," I casually responded, as I took a slice of ham and pineapple pizza and perched myself on the sofa next to Lena. "Are you serious!?" Miguel gasped in impassioned astonishment, as he swiftly grabbed the TV remote and put Simon Cowell on mute.

Miguel was a Spanish student residing from Barcelona and was currently in the UK studying fashion and design while also typically working part-time as a barista to afford the extortionate London rent. "Yep..." I sighed before eating the slice of pizza clasped in my hand. "He called me a Nazi and stomped off after I told him that I was Trump supporter," I murmured, as I unknowingly chewed loudly with my mouth open. "Oh my god... That's awful, George," exclaimed Sofia, as she looked at me with a hint of sadness in her eyes. Sofia was the second of the two Spaniards who were living in the house and seemed sincerely upset for me as she promptly put down her slice of pizza to wallow with me in my self-pity. "So, what are you going to do now?" questioned Lena, as I stared blankly at the muted image of Amanda Holden laughing hilariously at the sight of a ropey Michael Jackson impersonator attempting to moonwalk.

"I don't know... Kill myself maybe?" I quietly giggled, while reassuring myself to the fact that at least I had my dry British wit to pull me through the darkest of times. "How could you say something like that?" scolded Lena, who had completely not got the joke, as she cast her familiar stern gaze upon me. My British dry sense of humour was an acquired taste, as my attempt in poking fun at the whole Ronald scenario fell completely on deaf ears with the frowning and emotionless Pole, as Lena continued to intensely stare at me for any signs that I was on the verge of suicide.

"Why don't you message him?" suggested Miguel, as Sofia nodded her head in agreement. "Well, I would... but he has blocked me," I revealed, as I proceeded to take another slice of pizza and mourn in the sorrow of being blocked again by someone who was not willing to allow the existence of differing political opinions in their life.

Despite Ronald behaving in such an erratic and unacceptable manner, I didn't want to end things how they did, and upon getting off at Hackney Station, I proceeded to message him on WhatsApp – only to see an anonymous grey silhouette in place of where his display picture used to be.

It was then when I realised that there was no rationality in such irrational people and that I was probably better off to be rid of someone so angrily intolerant, but still, it did hurt a little. "Well, it's his loss," declared Sofia, as she perched herself up from the sofa and proceeded to hug me as she headed towards the bathroom. "Totally!" said Miguel in agreement. "If he can't accept you for your differences, why should he share your similarities with you?" It was rather ironic that Miguel was talking about differences between other people when he was in a fact a staunch socialist, however, it did give me assurance in the fact that not all people with opposing views were stark raving lunatics – even if Miguel did have a photo of United States Senator and socialist overlord Bernie Sanders as his mobile phone screensaver.

However, despite being a Bernie supporter, I knew that Miguel was right, as I perched myself up from the sofa and made my way towards my bedroom. Differences between people, whether that was a dissimilar interest in music or opposing football teams, shouldn't be a deciding factor when deciding on who to date. Unfortunately, when it came onto the subject of politics, it often was a deal-breaker that more often than not resulted in bitter disagreement and eventual separation.

However, what was even more frustrating for me was that someone having a non-identical political view didn't matter – in fact, I often welcomed it. I enjoyed hearing opposing views and conversing with those who held beliefs that were different from my own, even if those views were nuts. But with such division and hostility from those on the left, it was more usual to see antagonistic confrontation rather than civilised dialogue, especially when it came onto the subject of Trump.

I considered myself a very tolerant person, and like many conservatives, I was very respectful towards those with conflicting opinions. But seeing how abruptly Ronald had reacted towards me for simply being a Trump supporter had made me realise that maybe it was those who claimed to be the tolerant ones who were the actual fascists – as I swiftly crawled into my bed. "I hope I don't wake up tomorrow morning to see that you have cut your wrists," Lena warned, as she poked her head through my door to check to see that I wasn't in the process of committing suicide.

In the warmth of my bedsheets, as I cuddled up to my water bottle on what was a particularly cold night, my mind wandered as I thought about Ronald. I thought about Joey and Matthew and what Ronald was erratically telling them about me. No doubt I was being vividly portrayed as some kind of Trump sympathising antagonist, as Ronald recalled to his friend and cousin the unimaginable trauma that he had endured after finding himself unintentionally alone on a date with a villainous Nazi.

I had liked Ronald, and yet despite him being a total fruitcake, I wished that I was spending the night with him under the warmth of my bedsheets, instead of being in my bedroom alone with an IKEA water bottle tucked in between my nether regions. So, at that moment, with a water bottle firmly thrust in between my legs and feeling desperately lonely… I downloaded Tinder.

CHAPTER 5

STRONG, STABLE, AND READY TO MINGLE

Twenty-year-old vegan Marxist from Camden looking for a daddy with muscles and an income they can share with me" read the profile gazing back at me from my phone, as I swiftly swiped left without any hesitation. "Effeminate SJW feminist bottom looking for a masculine top to dominate me" read the next profile to flash before my screen, as I rapidly pressed my thumb down and proceeded to firmly swipe left as fast as I could. "I'm a socially nonconforming pansexual looking for a polyamorous relationship, ideally with a non-binary person who is sexually versatile and respects my pronouns and my need to wear knickers and heels and identify as a woman once a month" read the bio of the next profile that quickly followed suit, as a photo of someone whom I could only best describe as a dumpy man in suspenders and a blue wig flashed up on my phone screen. I had just downloaded Tinder, the dating app in which you were a mere swipe away from a match and a potential date with a genderless transsexual who insisted that you aggressively penetrate them midweek while calling them ma'am.

After exhausting my weary thumb with the amount of swiping that I was executing, I wondered if I had made a hasty decision in advertising myself on the digital dating meat market, especially as every profile that I was coming across belonged to either some kind of spindly social justice warrior or a toothless chav from the Jeremy Kyle Show. After Ronald had abruptly ended our date and berated me as a Nazi, I had become an emotional pile of feelings, which was ironic, considering that I often used to proudly state that facts didn't care about feelings. But the fact of the matter was that I was only human, and I had been made to feel like absolute shit about my political views and who I was as a person.

So, downloading Tinder and swiping right on budding twenty-year-old communists looking for love over avocado and toast as we discussed their liberal arts degree didn't exactly feel my heart with glee – on the contrary, it filled me with absolute dread and fear. It was a shame that it had come to this; after all, I always went out of my way to make sure that I did not exclude people based on their political affiliation or lack thereof.

But after the umpteenth time of being called a Nazi because I simply believed that the free market formula of supply and demand was a much better model than a socialist state – I had become greatly disheartened in trying to have a civilised conversation with so-called tolerant progressives. But the more I swiped left on Tinder, the more it seemed less likely that I would come across a Tory, or even someone of a sound mind, as I swiped past yet another profile that looked like they were more maniacal sociopath than boyfriend material.

However, instead of locking myself away in my bedroom and wallowing in victimhood and feeling sorry for myself, I embarked upon the new world of dating with an open mind and unlatched dreams with optimism and hopefulness, as I left behind the unfavourable memories of Ronald and went onto Tinder with the same conviction as Hillary Clinton in the 2016 United States presidential election - overly confident and deluded. But while there were certainly a lot of profiles to choose from, the vast array of profiles staring back at me with conveniently positioned airbrushed selfies filtered more times than Kim Kardashian's dimpled derriere left a to be desired.

And the ones who were not filtered beyond human recognition didn't exactly scream masculine either, quite the opposite actually, they screamed effeminate queen, and this was a major turn off. In a world in which the left wanted men to act like women, women to act like men, children to pick their gender, and men to ovate in the girl restrooms, I just wanted a man to be a man – simple! But as masculinity had gone the way of the dinosaurs and become extinct in recent years, the only options left for me to swipe on were poofs, queers, repugnant queens, and gay men with more hot air than a punctured tire. I just wanted a man, someone who you would look at without subconsciously thinking… 'Gay!'.

I wanted a masculine man, someone who was unapologetically unwomanly but who was also emotionally equipped to have an intellectual debate and see both sides of the equation. But instead, I was left with the typical riff-raff of womanish queers and leftist gays with annoyingly effeminate high-pitched voices that sounded more like a banshee letting off an ear wrenching scream than an actual virile voice of a man.

My thumb had just about grown tired of rapidly swiping left on Tinder when suddenly a profile stopped me dead in my tracks. "What do we have here?" I mumbled out loud to myself, as I gazed upon my phone screen in astonishment at the sight that had just appeared in my view. I had inadvertently stumbled across a profile of a man who, by a quick scan of their profile pictures, was not a pervert, polysexual or illegal immigrant wanting to scam me for a visa.

Did my eyes deceive me, I pondered, as I steadily scrolled down the bio section of this person who, so far, didn't appear to be a mentally unstable crackhead. Maybe I was acting prematurely, or maybe I was just excited to see a profile of a man who did not have three genders and a pierced nose, as I instantly swiped right and felt an immense feeling of accomplishment. I had just swiped right on my first Tinder profile, and if that wasn't a milestone within itself, we matched straight after.

It seemed that my normal-looking Tinder match liked me too, and within minutes, we were exchanging messages. "Hey there," he briskly messaged, as I excitedly swiped to my inbox. "You are hot!" he wrote, as I caught a glimpse of my beaming reflection staring back at me on my phone screen. Over the next few hours, we exchanged messages with one another in which we went back and forth while asking all the compulsory online dating questions that you would expect on a dating app, including casually enquiring if he had brutally mutilated anyone within the last six months.

After passing Tinder interrogation with flying colours, I bit the bullet and asked my match out on a date. A few days later and I found myself briskly making my way to meet my match on my first ever Tinder date – as I merrily skipped down the street as if I had just won the lottery. His name was Parker, a twenty-three-year-old fashion design student living in Wood Green. To be fair, I should have hastily blocked him as soon as he mentioned being a fashion design student and living in Wood Green, the kind of undesirable ghetto devoid of any cultural or economic benefits, however, as this was my first date since being politically dissected by Ronald, I figured I wasn't in the position to judge someone based on their unfortunate place of birth or the fact that they chose to study fashion. Despite the stereotypically gay choice of a college course and the fact that he lived in a shit hole, Parker seemed like a nice guy.

He had the most prepossessing cinnamon-brown eyes speckled with light hazel that I had ever seen, complete with a dark brown fuzzy beard that made him look like every bit the sexy lumberjack, as he posed behind the backdrop of Epping Forest wearing a red flannel shirt and flexing his arms in his display photo. To be honest, judging by the picture alone, he didn't come across as the kind of man who would spend their time sewing stitches and glueing on sequins in fashion design class. However, I was strictly on a no-judgment policy going into my first date with Parker, as I eagerly jumped onto the Piccadilly Line to meet him.

We had arranged to meet in Leicester Square just outside the Vue Cinema, and I felt a mixture of nerves and agitation as I made my way up the escalator of the station. As I darted out of Leicester Square station and made my way toward the direction of Shakespeare Water Fountain, I reached into my pocket and took out my phone to see what time it was.

I was ten minutes early, and Parker was nowhere to be seen, meaning that I could at least gather my bearings and check out my reflection in the nearby restaurant window to see if I looked like an absolute state on my first ever Tinder date. But before I could check to see if a strand of hair was out of place, my phone began to vibrate. "Hey, I'm here, where are you?" read the message, as Parker signalled his arrival.

Feeling panicky and apprehensive that Parker was within proximity, I frantically looked around the crowd of people gathered around Leicester Square while trying to see if I could spot the lumberjack with the red flannel shirt that had captured my attention on Tinder. And as I glanced around the bustling scene of self-indulgent tourists and zealous religious preachers condemning everyone to hell... there he was.

He looked exactly like his photo while I watched afar from the distance as he swiftly walked towards me. But as he began to draw closer, I noticed the faint sparkle of a single long dangling chainmail earring hanging from his left ear, as it swiftly swayed back and forth as he drew closer to me.

The beard and the red flannel shirt were present, but everything else was not exactly as I had imagined, as he reached out his arms to greet me. "Hey there," he smiled, as he proceeded to lean in and hug me, whilst I fixedly gazed at the swinging earing pierced in his ear. "Nice to meet you," I replied, as Parker leaned back while facing me – giving me time to now digest what exactly I was seeing before my eyes.

His face certainly looked the same, as did his brown eyes speckled with light hazel that was currently flickering at me under the rarity of the sun that had decided to make an appearance, however, there was something about Parker that I couldn't quite put my finger on. But as I looked past the wavering earing and prudently looked down at Parkers feet, it was then that my nagging concern became clear... Parker was wearing heels.

"So... erm... you didn't mention that you liked to wear heels on your profile," I remarked, as Parker stood there in five-inch red stilettos. "Oh, it's just a recent thing," Parker gushed, as he submissively shrugged his shoulders as if a man wearing heels wasn't such a big deal. "To be honest, I think that the whole concept of gender is just a social construct anyway, especially since I recently discovered that I was non-binary," Parker revealed, as I awkwardly gazed at the sight of a bearded man in a pair of heels standing across from me. Not only had I been catfished and misled by my Tinder date, but he had conveniently forgotten to mention the minor little detail that he was, in fact, a genderless alien with a fetish for big heels. The term 'non-binary' had in recent years become the latest leftist trend and buzzword in which men and women who claimed to not possess a gender instead referred to themselves as the non-gendered term of non-binary.

The singer Sam Smith, who had erratically bounced from being gay, then queer to finally settling on having no gender what so ever, was probably the most well-known person with the pronouns of 'they' and 'them' as they effeminately strutted around while complaining about oppression. And it looked like that Parker was going to follow suit with playing the non-binary oppressed victim, as they began to instruct me on how to refer to them in conversation as we began walking along the street.

"So, I would appreciate it if you respected my pronouns during the remainder of this date," insisted Parker, as I silently nodded in agreement while racking my brain on how I could make my excuses and flee. "What... like you respected me by misleading me to go on a date with you?" I fumed, as the sound of Parker's clanging heels echoed along the pavement of the street.

"I can't help how I identify," claimed Parker, as they looked at me with confusion as if casually identifying as non-binary was a normal occurrence. "Then perhaps next time you should have a disclaimer on your profile that states that you are prone to switching genders," I pointed out, as we abruptly halted outside a pub just off Shaftesbury Avenue.

"So... what now?" prompted Parker, as we stood outside the very patriotically titled Sir Winston Churchill Pub, as I envisioned the shock on Churchill's face if he knew that the men of his country that he had heroically led to victory during the second world war had now become genderless heel wearing non-binaries. "Listen... I'm sorry that I wasn't honest with you, this is all new me," Parker admitted, as I saw a glimmer of remorse in their non-gendered eyes, as they nervously twiddled with their pendulous earing that looked more like a drooping dream catcher than a genderless fashion accessory.

"I just want to be my authentic self and didn't think that you would want to meet me if you knew that I identified as non-binary," confessed Parker, as I aimlessly looked on with a look of perplexed bewilderment on my face. To be honest, I felt sorry for him (correction... them) as they sheepishly confessed their lack of understanding as to who they exactly were. True, someone who was a biological man who wore heels was not going to end up being my significant other anytime soon, but for someone to undergo an elaborate plan to catfish me in going out on a date with them, well – made me feel pretty chuffed actually. "Well, we're here now, we might as well make the best of it," I replied, as I set out to be more optimistic about the peculiar situation that I found myself in rather than standing in the cold with an extra-terrestrial genderless shapeshifter in five-inch heels.

We made our way through the wooden doors of the pub and into a room of hushed whispers and startled looks, as the sight of a bearded man walking along the stained floral carpet of the Sir Winston Churchill Pub was not the kind of sight the men and women of this traditionally working-class public house were accustomed to. "What can I get you, gentlemen?" asked the older bartender, as we perched up along the stalls of the bar.

Regrettably, in the swift act of foolishness in not being woke enough, the bartender had made the grave miscalculation of misgendering Parker, as an exasperated Parker scratched their beard and bestowed upon the elderly gentlemen a stern look of anger. "For your information, I do not use gender-based terminology and so would appreciate your cooperation if you would use non-discriminative dialogue when interacting with me," insisted a frowning Parker, as I uncomfortably watched on in embarrassment. "Sure, no problem," replied the bartender, as I internally breathed a sigh of relief that there wasn't going to be a gender showdown in the middle of the Sir Winston Churchill Pub. "So... What can I get you sir, and to you too... SIR?" snarled the barman, as Parker looked on in disbelief.

After Parker had gotten over the emotional turmoil of having been misgendered twice in the space of a minute, we grabbed our drinks and made our way to a lone table at the end of the pub where no further potential misgendering could occur. "I can't believe the nerve of that man!" fumed Parker, as they slurped down their pint of larger with all the manliness of a typical bloke down the pub, as I silently nodded my head in acknowledgement.

"How would he like it if he was misgendered?" seethed a still vexed Parker, as they firmly gripped their glass in tensed anger. "Well, technically, you misgendered him first as you didn't even ask what his preferred pronouns were in the first place," I pointed out, as Parker silently slurped on his beer and looked away.

We had been sitting in the pub for just over forty minutes, where I had so far downed two pints of Guinness and learnt that my non-binary date sitting across from me used to rummage through their mum's knickers draw when they were a teenager, and was also deathly afraid of Greggs sausage rolls, as they proceeded to tell me of the time that they almost 'died' after taking a bite of the insidious sausage meat wrapped in layers of crisp, golden puff pastry. "I was traumatised for life when the lady at Greggs served me a sausage roll after I had specifically requested a vegan sausage roll," recollected Parker, as they relived the painful memory of coming face to face with a non-vegan sausage roll. "I began to have heart palpitations and burst into tears after biting into it after realising that it contained meat," continued Parker, while also looking like they were on the verge of tears as if they were describing the after-effects of shellshock after landing on the shores of Normandy. As I sat and listened to Parker drone on about the flashbacks they had since endured over inadvertently eating a sausage roll, I realised that apart from being mentally unstable, non-binary Parker was a pretty boring person.

I would have thought that someone who existed outside of the gender spectrum of male and female would have more interesting things to talk about other than revealing that they were offended over Greggs sausage rolls, and then it dawned on me, people who identified as non-binary were pretty bland and monotonous people who had to go to the trouble of inventing an Imaginary new gender just to make themselves feel special and more interesting. "But you wouldn't understand my lived experience as you are a privileged cis-gendered white man," moaned Parker, as I looked on at them with an arched eyebrow and stern scepticism.

The term 'cis' was another buzzword from those on the left seemingly plucked from obscurity, in which a normal functioning human being who didn't 'identity' as a genderfluid squirrel was dubbed a cis, meaning someone who corresponds with their birth sex. According to non-binary Parker, being a homosexual gave me automatic 'minority' points, which meant that I was seemingly 'oppressed' enough to warrant a 'lived experience' while I painfully recounted my persecution and ill-treatment by villainous heterosexual people. However, because I was 'cis-gendered' and most importantly… white, I was deemed not oppressed enough to be considered truly a victim.

So, because my 'personal identity' and gender corresponded with my birth sex, I was oozing in entitled 'privilege' and would never be able to fully grasp the lived experience of minorities who were that little bit more oppressed than I was. So basically, because I didn't happen to be a transsexual intergalactic flying hippopotamus, I was simply far too privileged to fathom the struggle that Parker had to endure in being a bearded man who publicly wore heels – as imaginary violins began to string chords of victimhood around the non-binary persecuted minority sitting across from me. After the umpteenth time of hearing the self-loathing victimhood of living in a binary society by Parker, I was itching to make my excuses and leave.

But being the painfully polite Englishman that I was, I begrudgingly bit that upper lip and soldered on with this disaster of a date that I found myself on, as I proceeded to quietly nod along to my non-binary's woeful tales of the apparent struggle of being a non-conforming genderless entity in which non-vegan sausage rolls sinisterly lurked behind every corner. However, after enduring another tedious hour of pronouns, privilege and self-pity, I finally found the strength from within to break with social courtesy and put an end to my suffering. But before we left the binary confines of the Sir Winston Churchill Pub, Parker had to use the toilet.

I found it amusing that even a non-binary person who existed in a universe in which gender was just a concept of infinite possibilities – Parker still had to use the toilet, as I watched with great interest to see which restroom they would choose to urinate in. I waited at our table and watched from afar as if I was gazing upon a wild animal in an unnatural habitat while Parker strutted in their heels and made their way towards the toilets.

I could imagine Sir David Attenborough narrating the whole scenario as I waited with bated breath to see where Parker would eventually choose to urinate. "And here we have a strange and peculiar creature who identifies as nothing," Attenborough would articulate through the TV, as viewers watched in amazement as the non-binary organism navigated the binary trials in deciding where to pee. Being a non-binary lifeforce of boundlessness identities, I almost imagined a portal would materialize out of nowhere for

Parker to enter and take a dump in, but lo and behold, just as I got excited over the possibility of alien life appearing, Parker conformed to the genitalia that was steadily dangling in between their legs and proceeded to enter the binary dimension of the male restroom. What an anti-climax!

"It was lovely meeting you," smiled Parker, as they proceeded to give me a faint and emasculated pat on the back outside Leicester Square Station. "You too," I replied with as much enthusiasm as a door knob, while knowing full well that I would never willingly go out of my way to see them again, unless of course I magically conjured up their genderless spirit by chanting their name into a mirror as if I was performing a satanic ritual to cleanse myself of the shame of being seen in public with them.

CHAPTER 6

MAN, I FEEL LIKE A WOMAN

I always found it ironic that the ones who claimed to be tolerant and who paraded around the word diversity like a hooker advertising their services were not as open to the diversity of differing opinions that did not conveniently conform to their own echoed leftist ideology. Being ghosted for liking Trump or for being a Brexiteer had become as normal as spraying body deodorant on my sweaty armpits before a night out.

Any sniff of Trumpism that my snuffling date could smell other than the smell of my cheap cologne from Boots would be enough to send them into a paralytic state of Trump derangement syndrome. But despite being repeatedly labelled a Nazi from those who worked themselves into a state of madness over my political leanings, I never once thought that being conservative somehow made me some kind of authoritarian ultranationalist. On the contrary, I always assumed that it just made me rational and well-reasoned.

To me, conservatism said what it did on the tin, and that was to promote traditional values and ideas against the opposition of radical change. However, it wasn't just my political views or the fact that I wanted to converse common sense that was seemingly the only problem, but the fact that I dared to be conservative and homosexual at all that was the key issue that defied all expectations from those who peddled identity politics for political gain.

According to the left, as a gay man living in London, I was expected to excitedly support child drag queens sexually gyrating in the local drag kids contest, while volunteering at the local mosque on the weekend to promote intercommunity diversity, all while wearing a rainbow-coloured jock-strap and waving my rainbow flag manically in the air whilst trying to convince a 108-year-old Islamic scholar that they could self-identify as a crippled Jamaican woman with a colossal backside under the guise of genderfluidity.

My sexuality had foredoomed my destiny, and, as a result, I was forced to be just another oppressed minority statistic on the Labour Party policy manifesto while the political left salivated over my homosexual carcass for their political advantage. Having my sexuality exploited as a political prop was always awkward, especially when my sexuality was neither part of my identity nor relevant to my social and political views.

For me, my sexuality (which I didn't choose or have a choice over) did not regulate or form my political perspective in any way, shape, or form. And while effeminate homosexual men flocked to Beyoncé like she was Jesus with a weave, I was at home binge watching Margaret Thatcher parliamentary debates on YouTube. Having views that did not conform to my fellow homosexual brethren greatly limited my chances of getting past the initial WhatsApp stage, let alone getting an actual first date. And if I did somehow successfully pass the filtering stage without being outed as a Tory, then the date would always somehow end in disaster.

It had almost become a regular occurrence to witness a seemingly normal-looking man quickly turn into a raging venomous queen – angrily typing in capitals that I was an apparent 'traitor' to the LGBT community, a community that I wasn't even aware that I was a member of, and all because I had casually mentioned in conversation that I had previously voted for former Conservative Party MP Ann Widdecombe on Celebrity Big Brother.

From my experience, it seemed that for one perfectly sane homosexual man, nine malevolent queers were telling you to hand back in your 'gay card' or face excommunication from the church of queer – and all because you had made the outrageous statement that women don't have penises. And while the LGBT community continued to fill its ranks with mix and match interchangeable genitals and adults with an unhealthy infatuation with children, there was also the new breed of miscellaneous gender identities like Parker who didn't have a clue as to what body part inconveniently positioned itself between their legs.

Speaking of imaginary delusion, it had been a whole week since I had experienced my first interaction with a non-binary person. And after narrowly avoiding public ridicule for the rest of my life in the Sir Winston Churchill Pub, I wasn't expecting to hear back from Parker after the catastrophe that was our first date. So, when I unexpectedly received a message from Parker on WhatsApp asking me out on another date, I was confused, especially when the last time I had seen non-binary Parker, they had reluctantly conformed to the restraint of gender-stereotypes of a binary society by peeing in the urinals of the men's toilets. There was not a physical attraction on my part towards the non-specified gendered person with the dangling earing, with the likelihood of a blossoming romance developing as unlikely to happen as Hillary Clinton becoming President of the United States. Yet, despite what was a pretty abysmal first date, I agreed to meet up with Parker again – if not more so for the fact that I had absolutely nothing else planned for the day. I arrived for my second date with Parker as I waited upon the arrival of my non-conforming companion outside Nando's in Oxford Circus, where the tantalizing smell of chicken butterflies seduced me like Harvey Weinstein enticing an opportunist out of work actress on the casting couch.

I gazed upon the bustling crowds of people walking along the concrete pavements as I tried to spot the same swaying chandelier earing that had blinded my vision the last time that we had met. However, as I dreary looked up from my phone and spiritlessly scanned my surroundings, I spotted someone or something that vaguely resembled Parker slowly walking towards me, except this time, the strut had a little more sass in the hips. As everyone within close proximity paused in disbelief as the sashaying figure made their way towards me, I glimpsed upon a familiar dangling earring swinging loosely with each step. "Hey hun," greeted the lisping voice now standing in front of me, as I confusingly gaped at the person looking back at me. I couldn't quite put my finger on who this person was and why they were standing within touching distance as their hand gripped their tilted hip. But then, it suddenly dawned on me, the person wearing a long white floaty dress with a long flowing mane of hair while clutching a blue leathered handbag was in fact... Parker.

For someone who was supposedly genderless and exempt from socially engineered gender roles, Parker was sure looking every bit the woman right about now, minus the bushy beard and conspicuous Adam's apple, as I stared on in bewilderment. "Erm... Parker?" I tentatively asked as I peered fixedly at the brightly coloured red lips and green shadowed eyes looking back at me. "Oh, my name is not Parker any more hun," they abruptly announced, while swiftly yanking up the skin coloured tights strained around their gangly hairy legs. "Huh?" I gasped in confusion, while still looking on in disbelief at the unusual sight seductively pouting back at me. "I've changed my name to Paula," they revealed, while timely flicking their rickety wig over their shoulders in a vainglorious manner.

In the space of a week, Parker had gone from genderless nobody to towering transsexual and was now standing outside Nando's wearing a wig that looked like it had seen much better days. "I figured that being non-binary was just an evolutionary phase towards my real being," proclaimed the newly christened Paula, as they flashed a defiant smile on their bristling face. "Oh, OK... So, are you hungry?" I hastily murmured, as I briskly moved the conversation from gender to chicken, so to avoid a long and drawn-out conversation about the gender spectrum before I had even had a bite to eat.

"Table for two?" asked the waitress, as she led us to our table and through the gawking sight of puzzled diners staring at Paula as they strutted through the restaurant as if Naomi Campbell had just casually popped out for a cheeky Nando's.

While me and the former Parker, who was now calling themselves by the name of Paula looked through the menu, I promptly brought the subject back onto the gender spectrum of infinity and beyond, as I tried to establish just what Paula's new pronouns were in case I inadvertently put my foot in my mouth and said something that I wasn't supposed to.

"I use the pronouns she and her, and I have also hopped onto the menstrual cycle," gushed Paula, while also apparently being able to defy all biological normalities by having a bleeding vagina develop between her legs overnight. While I certainly didn't want to intentionally offend Paula, who looked and sounded happier than the gloomy Parker, I was afraid of the ramifications if I accidental did use the 'he' word, as I timidly looked across at the bearded figure sitting across from me who now wanted to be referred to as a woman. And while I had no problem in being polite, I was petrified that I would mistakenly forget to use the correct pronouns and trigger an emotional reaction, as I sat across from the broad-shouldered Paula as she desperately tried to succinctly sip on her glass of water with all the womanliness of a genetic man who unashamedly identified themselves as non-binary only a week prior. Parker had seemingly jumped ship from the passive non-binary community to the transgender community, a relentless community who was a much more aggressive and militant operation than their non-gendered counterparts.

As the trans agenda continued to escalate and surge, it wasn't just concerned women being attacked by biological men in dresses and being labelled as 'transphobic' that had become a worrying epidemic in recent years, as tyrannical trannies actively sought to criminally prosecute anyone who did not idly conform to their authoritarian undemocratic rule under their slanted heeled stilettos.

Would I be aggressively dragged out of Nando's kicking and screaming as the national pronoun law enforcers promptly throw the legal book at me for the unfathomable hate crime of 'deadnaming' Paula as I begin my strenuous jailtime locked up behind bars sharing a cell with Barry the serial rapist who self-identifies as Barbara on the weekend.

In recent years, deadnaming had become the malicious act of referring to a transgender person's birth name instead of their chosen name of Crystal or Buttercup, whether intentionally done or not, and could land those who referred to Caitlyn Jenner as the formerly identified Bruce an instantaneous ban on Twitter for the rest of their life. And while I wasn't purposely looking to deadname Paula, I sure didn't want to find myself permanently erased on social media for mistakenly referring to a biological male as their certified sex either, especially as sitting across from Paula it was obvious that her mannish table manners were as unladylike as Phil Mitchell.

With a million questions racing through my head over the absurdity of somehow ending up being on a second date with a reformed non-binary genderless entity who now identified as a menstruating transsexual woman in the space of a week, and not to mention being crippled with severe hunger pains and anxiety in not wanting to carelessly deadname my date, I proceeded to order our food at the counter. Upon returning to the table with cutlery and drinks in hand, I proceeded to diverge into Paula's newfound identity, as I quizzed her on how she had come to the resolution that she had been a woman all along.

"I just woke up last week and felt like a woman," shrugged Paula, as she casually sipped on her glass of water while her manicured pinkie pointed needle-like in the air. "So, I assume that the next step for you will be to undergo surgical reassignment?" I questioned, as the waiter placed our dishes onto the table. "No, I don't feel that the genitalia in between my legs defines my womanhood," replied Paula, who had also miraculously been cured of her irrational fear of meat, as she proceeded to take a bite out of her lemon and herb chicken breast, which may or may not have identified as an ovulating woman in its previous life before being skinned, deep-fried, and promptly consumed.

"So, let me get this straight," I reasoned, as I confusingly pondered over the convoluted gender labyrinthine that I found myself trawling in. "You were born a boy, then you self-identified as non-binary, and now you are suddenly a woman called Paula who has a penis?" I questioned, before taking a swift gulp of Pepsi from the glass gripped in my hand. "Pretty much," smirked Paula, as if changing gender and sex was as casual as changing bed sheets. While self-identifying as a woman was just a carefree move for Paula – who was still physically and biological a man, for women who were biological females (with actual functioning menstrual cycle) men casually identifying as women meant men with penises being able to access women's and girls' private single-sex spaces such as toilets, changing rooms and female prisons under the guise of exclusivity. And while it was now deemed normal for men with penises who self-identified as a woman to share a shower with a biological woman in a changing room, any woman who raised their concern over having to share their shower gel with self-identifying transsexual women whilst their 'female penises' flapped about like a hallucinating snake were aggressively labelled as a 'TERF'.

The term TERF, which was an acronym for 'trans-exclusionary radical feminist' had become a derogatory and disparaging word used to insult biological women by antagonized and often unhinged transgender activists and members of the LGBT community who had become squirrelly deranged in their pursuit to eradicate biological women from public spaces – all for the sake of diversity and tolerance no less. It was also rather ironic that these were actual biological men in dresses hurling venomous abuse at women, as feminists who wore pink beanie hats resembling ugly vaginas on their heads sat idly by and done nothing for fear of offending men who were now self-identifying as women. While Paula, who I assumed did not want to start competing in women's weightlifting competitions any time soon self-identified as a woman overnight, she was also quite clearly still a man, in every sense of the word.

I always found it hard to get my head around the fact that men who 'transitioned' into women almost always ended up portraying themselves as overly feminised versions of women – as if their only perception of what made a woman a 'woman' merely consisted of cliché generalisations of womanly and overly feminised traits such as long hair, make-up, perfectly manicured nails, big lips, and even bigger breasts. While these stereotypical attributes were a socially engineered construct according to those on the left, it was always rather telling that men who suddenly became women overnight always ended up looking excessively feminised in their look and appearance – or at least tried their best in playing the part. And despite Paula's insistence that she was now miraculously a biological woman who had morning cramps and a pack of trusty tampons in her handbag, the fact of the matter was that Paula was still biologically a male, despite her being able to fit into a pretty dress that was four sizes too small.

While I was happy in being respectful towards someone eating peri chicken sitting across from me, that didn't mean that I had to suspend reality and indulge in a belief or delusion that simply was not based in fact. As the European waiter returned to collect our plates, both of which had been completely devoured by testosterone appetite, our unassuming minimum wage worker found themselves in the awkward dilemma of how to address the diners on their table, especially as one of them just looked like a man in a wig and dress.

The anticipation was palpable as I waited with bated breath to see how the confused waiter would address Paula, who was now adamant that she was a biological woman. "Can I get you, gentlemen, anything else?" politely asked the waiter, while unbeknownst to him committing the most consequential of crimes by misgendering someone who had just recently changed their sex, as I looked on at Paula for a reaction while anxiously waiting for signs of the apocalypse to commence. "No, that's all, thanks," calmly replied Paula, as she smiled to the waiter who nippy walked off with our plates in hand.

That was it? I thought to myself, as Paula contently sipped on the last drop of her water without any fuss or fluster. I was half expecting the polar ice caps to deteriorate into melted ice cubes after the rage of being misgendered, but instead, there was nothing but the sound of waves gently drenching the shores as Paula looked over at me and smiled. For someone who was supposedly doing erratic spins on the menstrual cycle, Paula was eerily calm after being labelled as a gentleman, which was even more remarkable considering that non-binary Parker had exploded in pronoun pique a week earlier in the Sir Winston Churchill Pub after being 'misgendered' by an older gentleman who had probably no idea what a non-binary person even was.

While I did think that Paula, who was now apparently a discharging woman was absolutely stark-raving mad, I respected the fact that she didn't cause a scene over being referred to as the biological sex in which they were born as in the middle of Nando's.

Amid gender and gonads, a topic that I had yet to bring up to Paula was the subject of politics, and despite what normally would occur when I casually injected politics into the conversation on a date, I was itching to know her political stance, considering that she had changed her identity more times than Anna Soubry had changed her political party. "So, what are your thoughts on Brexit?" I quizzed Paula, as I clenched my fingers firmly onto the side of the table in anticipation of her answer. "I think it's great," smiled Paula, as I proceeded to pick my jaw up from off the floor in utter incredulity.

To be honest, I had half expected the usual "Brexiteers are racist" babble that I had grown accustomed to hearing when bringing up the subject of Brexit to strangers I had met online, but instead, I found myself sitting across from a gender-fluid shapeshifter in Nando's who had also voted to leave the European Union.

In what parallel universe did I wake up in when a cross-dressing man agreed with my political perspective? This was new territory for me as I proceeded to tread with caution as I diverged deeper into the political mind of someone who up until now, I had regulated to the looney bin. "So, did you vote in the 2019 European elections?" I asked as I gulped down the last drops of Pepsi in my glass. "Yes, I voted for the Brexit Party," revealed Paula, as she nimbly adjusted her flimsy wig.

Not only was I currently existing in a warped parallel universe with somebody who changed their gender and sex as promptly as ordering a Big Mac, but someone who also had voted for a Party in which Nigel Farage and Ann Widdecombe were both at the helm. Now, if only Paula could morph back into Parker, ditch the dress and heels, take a lesson in masculinity one on one, hit the weights, and take out the George Michael earing, then maybe, just maybe, this second date could blossom into a potential civil partnership. And then it dawned on me, I had unfairly judged Paula in assuming that she would be a lunatic leftie based on her mix-match of gender identities, in the same way that many had assumed that I had a Jeremy Corbyn shrine tucked away in my closet because of my sexuality.

True, she was unbalanced when it came to the direction that she swung on the gender spectrum, but when it came to political opinions, she was of pretty sound mind. After we had put Brexit to bed, I then proceeded to tell Paula of my issues in dating and the unwavering difficulties that my political point of view had given me when it came to trying to find a boyfriend who didn't think that being conservative made me the spawn of Satan. She nodded in agreement and began to tell me the complexity of her metamorphosing gender identity and how her political position found her being at odds with those she once thought were close friends. "After my friends found out that I was a Brexiteer, they deleted me from social media completely," sighed Paula, as she shared with me the sadness of losing people she once loved because of differing political opinions. I nodded my head in empathy as I recalled the moment I woke up one morning after going on a political Facebook rant to find out that I had been digitally erased on social media for my political leanings. Friends of mine, close friends that I had grown up with had removed me from their friend list, and all because I had committed the heinous crime of publicly sharing a political Facebook status that they had seemingly not agreed with. It's safe to say that like many of my dates who had promptly removed themselves from our table, I never saw those friends again.

"I remember telling my best friend Samuel that I would be voting for Theresa May and the Conservative Party in the 2017 general elections," recalled Paula, as she gently twiddled with her hanging earring while entranced in a saddened gaze. "He told me that I was an absolute fucking disgrace for voting for a party that had introduced section 28," Paula continued, as her eyelids began to softly flicker.

"We ended up having a huge row, and we never saw each again after that," Paula concluded, as she took a deep breath and exhaled over reliving a moment that was still painful to bear – seemingly even more painful than recollecting the time she inadvertently bit into a Greggs sausage roll. While not as overly conservative as many on the political right, it seemed that Paula's political perspective still posed a problem for those who claimed to embrace diversity and tolerance, the same people who sneered at the diversity of differing opinions, especially when it did not conform to their monolithic agenda. Regardless or not if a person was homosexual, lesbian, or a non-binary transparent liquefied shapeshifter who blossomed into a transwoman overnight – if they didn't have the subscribed political views, then they were truly never oppressed and diverse enough to begin with.

Being with Paula was a very different experience than being on a date with Parker, and even though for all intents and purposes, both Paula and Parker were genetically and biologically the same person, I noticed a spring in her confidence – even if the heels had slightly less inch to them than the ones that Parker had worn. And while I had no problem with consensual adults who found themselves suffering with the lingering mismatch between their biological sex and their gender identity who went on to undergo surgical reassignment to help with their gender dysphoria condition, I made no secret of the fact that I was against the trans agenda that the LGBT community continued to perpetuate in schools, along with the indoctrination of mass castration of prepubescent boys who were taught to believe that they were born into the wrong body simply because they just so happened to be slightly effeminate compared to the other boys in their class.

Child transgenderism had become a major pandemic in recent years with a growing number of adults revealing later on in life their deep regret in having undergone gender-reassignment surgery after realising that they did not have gender dysphoria after all but instead had been encouraged and coerced to do so during an impressionable age when they didn't even know the difference between plasticine and puberty, let alone understand the complexity and medical repercussions of undergoing surgical reassignment.

But regardless of my views, I also had no problem with eating spicy chicken with a biological man in a dress who self-identified as a woman. Paula wasn't trying to round up little boys like the child catcher and lock them in cages before injecting them with puberty blockers with the depraved intent of castrating their testicles and wearing them as earrings. On the contrary, Paula was just living her authentic life and I could respect that. And being the deferential English gentlemen, I even used her preferred pronouns, even if she did have more facial stubble than the yeti.

CHAPTER 7

100 GENDERS LATER

After I got home from spending the day with the newly self-identified Paula, I couldn't stop thinking about the concept of gender and the notion that people could change their gender and sex on a whim depending on how they were feeling on that particular day.

One day you could be a regular heterosexual man with a job and a mortgage and… poof! – you were now a woman who still suffered from the crippling effects of man flu. But while the sound of gender-swapping sounded fun on paper, it didn't help matters in my lingering relationship woes, especially when all I wanted to do was meet someone who didn't have an interchangeable cock.

Circulating the dating scene scouting for one gender was hard enough, but trying to meet a potential significant other when there were an array of multiple genders to navigate through on Tinder was virtually impossible, especially when the men I liked always turned out to be transmuting life forces with the ability to shapeshift their penis into a pineapple. According to the BBC, the British public service and apparent impartial and unbiased broadcaster, there were at least 100 genders to choose from. So, if you woke up feeling like a hamster with boobs or a non-binary asteroid, then chances are that you'll probably find the right identity for you out there somewhere in the universe of limitless genders and possibilities. However, if like me and you only identified as a mere homosexual male with the pronouns of, he and him, then it was highly unlikely that you would appear as exciting on Tinder next to a gender-nonconforming queer whose preferred pronouns transcend space and time itself.

I could just about cope with the fact that we lived in a world that had gone utterly bonkers, however, what was difficult in living amongst madness was when people insisted that you indulge in their madness with them. But despite merely being an inferior male and having private parts that did not transform upon request, I was energised and ready to go on another date – ideally with a fellow male who didn't think that he was a menstruating woman.

While I appreciated making a friend in Paula, I didn't download Tinder to make acquaintances with transgender Brexiteers. So, I proceeded to go where any logical and sound minded dater would venture during these crazed times of confusing genders, pronouns, and imaginative periods, I went onto Tumblr. Yes, Tumblr; that digital safe space on the world-wide-web that had eradicated all traces of porn and nudity and was the home to jaded millennials and the emotionally unhinged demographic of Generation Z who skulked on the deepest darkest pages of this obscure microblogging platform of progressive ideas and queer anarchism – wallowing in commiseration and self-pity while blaming their failures in life on the 'social patriarchy' that had oppressed them throughout their entire eighteen years' worth of life.

This was also the perfect place to find out all about the miscellaneous array of genders and identities that had evolved under the imagination of diversity and inclusiveness. A deep dive into the pits of Tumblr and I was met with the strangest sights and peculiar imagery that I had ever seen, but it was paramount that I emerged myself with the strange and unusual so that I could learn about the strange and unusual, and avoid swiping right and going on a date with someone whose gender was merely questionable reality.

It seemed that in my interaction with Parker and Paula, the concept of gender and sex had evolved beyond my comprehension and that I was merely a little cis-gendered male desperately gasping for air in an ocean of metamorphosing entities. So, to be cautious when approaching these strange and peculiar individuals, I developed a survivor guide seized from the very depths of Tumblr. This survivor guide would not only help me identify these unidentified beings on Tinder but to also let me know how to react if I found myself isolated and alone on a date with a miscellaneous unspecified lifeform who had just abruptly announced that they identified as a genderfluid toothbrush as we ordered our drinks.

I painstakingly studied these social justice warriors very own native language and translated their meaning as if I was studying prehistoric paintings in cave dwellings from ancient times and came up with my very own definition of each one of the specified genders on the gender spectrum. So, the next time that I saw 'gender-questioning' on a Tinder profile, I wouldn't mistake it for the name of a science fiction film and excitedly swipe right in haste.

Asexual – More likely to get a blowjob from a decaying corpse then a frigid asexual.

Female to Male Trans Man – Phalloplasty penis is an acquired taste – like Marmite and Jameela Jamil.

Female to Male Transgender Man – And just like that, vaginal itchiness was a thing of the past.

Female to Male Transsexual Man – Will probably end up looking like Ellen DeGeneres post-surgery.

F2M – A lazy abbreviated way in stating that you were allegedly born with the wrong sexual organs.

Gender-neutral – A politically correct term for a cross dresser.

Hermaphrodite – Genital civil war.

Intersex Man – I miss the good old days of Woolworths when the only 'pick and mix' to choose from were cola bottles and jelly beans, not chromosomes and genitals.

Intersex Person – Incomprehensible and difficult to translate at the best of times, a bit like a mumbling Nancy Pelosi.

Intersex Woman – Is there any difference between an intersex man or an intersex woman? Asking to phone a friend.

Male to Female Trans Woman – Still extremely offended that they don't have a womb and cannot fight systemic sexism and get an abortion.

Male to Female Transgender Woman – Prone to break out in an enraged testosterone temper if you inadvertently misgender them.

Male to Female Transsexual Woman – Part man, part woman, but still has a penis tucked in between their legs.

Man – An extinct species by the year 2050.

M2F – Again, another lazy and abbreviated way to state that you are quite possibly some kind of morbidly obese Romanian transsexual prostitute.

Polygender – Probably has no friends and spends their time alone doing Buzzfeed quizzes.

T* Man – Who the fuck would assign themselves as a T* man and still expect to be taken seriously in a civilised society?

T* Woman – This could be the name of the latest feminist femme fatal who goes around fighting the patriarchy by destroying sexist white men with her laser-shooting pussy. But, in reality, is more likely just another paunchy social justice warrior who insists that you use their preferred pronouns or else you get called a Nazi.

Two* Person – Two gender-confused people for the price of one?

Two-Spirit Person – A person who is most likely possessed by some sort of demon summoned by US Senator and indigenous Indian tribal woman Elizabeth Warren who now wants her stolen land back. A bit like the exorcist, just eco-friendlier.

Woman – Otherwise known as a menstruator.

Agender – An extraterrestrial life form that holds the extraordinary ability of possessing no distinctive gender and not having to pee like the rest of us mere cis-mortals.

Androgyne – Can be seen late at night sticking needles into Donald Trump voodoo dolls.

Aporagender – A gender that cannot be grasped or be comprehend and so is best left ignored and alone.

Androgynes – Don't you dare call them male or a female. They are a socially non-conforming entity that exists only in the furthest reaches of the mind and can only be seen by using thermal imaging system technology.

Androgynous – This gender identity is indeterminate of sex and can only be seen with a little bit of pixie dust and a lot of imagination.

Bigender – Literally translated as 'two genders' or 'double gender'. So basically, conjoined twins who have to pee from the same penis.

Butch – Most likely a mannish lesbian who dons a strap on to assert her dominant presence in the bedroom.

Cis – Is immune to all suffering and oppression according to the left.

Cis Female – The nurse saw a little vagina in between the baby's legs, the nurse ticked the girl box on the birth certificate.

Cis Male – The nurse saw a little penis in between the baby's legs, the nurse ticked the boy box on the birth certificate.

Cis Man – Literally the devil reincarnated and the reason for all death, poverty, and lingering misery on the planet. Well, according to the profound philosophy of nose pierced feminists anyway.

Cis Woman – Has a tendency to make false rape accusations.

Cisgender – Most likely a literate hippy with a god complex.

Cisgender Female – A cis woman who doesn't want to use the term 'woman' as it has 'man' in the word which makes it sexiest, so prefers to be called cisgender female, even though female has the term 'male' in the word which is also a male synonym. Go figure.

Cisgender Man – Made from dust by God / Zeus / Odin and the 28,000,000 other deities in his / her / their image.

Cisgender Male – Disappearing as fast as Madeleine McCann.

Cisgender Woman – Made from the rib of Adam, but still ended up with the dimpled backside of Kim Kardashian.

Demi Boy – A long-distance relative of the Myspace emo.

Demi Girl – A popular gender identity among chubby teenage girls with green hair and severe depression.

Demisexual – A person who only experiences sexual attraction after forming a strong emotional connection with a partner. So pretty much like most people, minus the constant need for victimhood.

Enby – A gender which is profound, deep-rooted and far-reaching, and also most likely to get on your last nerve.

Female to Male – If all biological cis men inherited traits of 'toxic masculinity' from conception, did this mean that women who transitioned into men would also automatically develop toxic masculinity as a result of rapidly injecting themselves with male testosterone? This was the type of extensive and profound question that had left many historical scholars still pondering.

FTM – If you can't be bothered to use the full adjective of your new gender, then why in the hell should your preferred pronouns even be acknowledged?

Femme – A generic and overly effeminate white homosexual man who deludedly thinks that he is the reincarnation of Sasha Fierce in a pair of Primark jeans.

Fluidflux – The kind of person who insists that you check your privilege because of your gender while having no idea as to what gender they actually are themselves.

Foxkin – A person who identifies both spiritually and physically as having the traits of an animal and therefore should probably be incapacitated by a tranquillizer dart rather than swiping right on Tinder.

Gender Fluid – A bit like interchangeable IKEA furniture.

Genderflux – A gender that changes and adapts to other genders around it. Similar to a chameleon, but without the virtue signalling and cancel culture.

Gender Nonconforming – Doesn't want to conform to a binary society but will still stand when taking a piss at the men's urinals.

Genderless – Unable to be seen unless you are intoxicated or off your head on crystal meth.

Gendervoid – The life and soul of the party.

Gender Questioning – Something who approaches gender the way they approach a free Netflix subscription trial, still questioning...

Gender Variant – A metamorphosis life form who can't quite decide if they are an apple tree or a flowery bush. Either way, they won't be coming close to my bush anytime soon.

Genderqueer – Probably a vegan, probably a member of Antifa, and probably needs a good wash.

Greygender – A person who identifies as partially outside the gender binary and who lingers in the grey area of uncertainty. So basically – one leg in and one leg out but still can't make up their fucking mind as to which gender they want to fully commit to.

Genderglitch – A glitch in the matrix and a result of a lapse in the space-time continuum that has produced a gender in which reality cannot quite be explained. Also, probably a stoner.

Intersex – A demonic mythological creature and quite possibly fictitious, like incestuous Somalian export Ilhan Omar.

Male to Female – Used to be called Chris, now goes by the name of Chardonnay.

MTF – Another incredibly lazy way to state that you have gender dysphoria and severe mental health issues.

Maverique – Described as being completely independent of male, female, and neutral genders but still stamps their foot and demands to use the ladies changing rooms.

Microgender – A gender that is so minute and small you actually need a microscope just to be able to see them. A bit like most penises that I have unfortunately encountered.

Neither –More likely someone who is neither interesting and nor someone you would want to spend a considerable amount of time with.

Neutrois – Quite possibly some kind of space-age galactic warlord from a 1950's science fiction comic. But most likely just someone with an overactive imagination and too much time on their hands.

Non-binary – Has become a bit of a fad in recent years, a bit like Tamagotchi and Black Lives Matter.

Non-gendered – Must be a lonely place when you have no boxes to tick on the equality form.

Neurogender – A gender that is linked to the mental illness and neurological conditions of a person. Well, at least they are being honest with the fact that they are absolutely bat shit crazy.

Other – Quite possibly a long distant relative of the dementor from the Harry Potter series.

Quoigender – Someone who believes that gender is inaccessible and inapplicable but will still accept accessible handouts from the government.

Pangender – Potentially a psychopath or a member of the Scottish National Party, but in all honestly, most likely to be both.

Polygender – A gender identity which is conveniently translated as 'many genders'. Useful if you have commitment issues and are most likely to cheat.

Postgender – A gender that was discovered post the prehistoric age but has since been made extinct along with the dinosaurs and Barack Obama.

Trans – It's a bird...it's a plane… no, it's just gender dysphoria.

Trans Female – Was assigned the wrong gender at birth by an NHS Nurse exported from Eastern Europe who couldn't tell the difference between a penis and a vagina and is now suffering from the long-term mental distress of being 'misgendered' and now wants sympathy and financial compensation.

Trans Male – I think this is a woman who thinks that she is a man. Or is it a man who thinks that he is a woman? At this point, who the fuck knows!

Trans Man – Overcompensates for their lack of testosterone by drinking beer and acting like a lad.

Trans Person – They find baby gender reveals offensive because gender is a social construct, yet undergoes surgery to modify their genitalia to conform to said socially constructed gender.

Trans*Female – Wears their castrated testicles as knuckle dusters.

Trans*Male – The result of being anally probed by aliens.

Trans*Man – The only way to close the notorious gender pay gap is to become a woman while still keeping your male sexual organs firmly tucked in between your legs.

Trans*Person – A transcendental intergalactic being that exists outside of the reality of the limitations of our consciousness.

Trans*Woman – Someone who believes that children should be able to chemically castrate themselves.

Transsexual – Still ends up looking like Rosie O'Donnell.

Transsexual Female – Thinks that all men are sexist so changes their gender to break the misogynist hierarchy. Stunning and brave.

Transsexual Male – They have a prosthetic penis and they aren't afraid to whack you over the head with it too if you fail to conform.

Transsexual Man – Quite possibly a hallucination.

Transsexual Person – Wants to change their gender to the opposite sex but does not want to be gender labelled in the process.

Transsexual Woman – The kind of intensely confused person to complain about patriarchal attitudes and gender stereotypes, yet tries their best to act as feminine as possible.

Transgender Female – Most likely to think that everything white is abhorrent and racist, including snow and semen.

Transgender Person – Feels trapped in the wrong body but is not sure what body they want to transition into so will settle for being neither male nor female but happily exist somewhere in the middle.

Two-Spirit – Proof that Unicorns do exist.

Transfeminine – Anything with 'trans' and 'feminine' in the same sentence is highly unlikely to receive a swipe from me on Tinder.

Transmasculine – A bodybuilder in a pink tutu? At this point, who the fuck knows!

Ungender – Described as a gender that can one day be clear and understanding, and the next day is confused and disconcerted. So pretty much like most women during the menopause.

Venufluid – A gender that sounds more like something that can be found lurking on the bottom of the toilet.

Virgender – A gender that is particularly genderless due to stress, which is pretty ironic considering that trying to remember imaginary preferred pronouns is giving me nothing but stress.

Xenogender – According to the profound philosophy of Tumblr, this is a gender that cannot be contained and understood by mere human perception. What! So, you are telling me that the other imaginary and fictitious genders on this list are actually comprehensible!?

X-Gender – An additional form of the 'genderqueer identity' but sounds more like a scientific experiment gone wrong.

XTX – Another term of the intersex condition which means that technically they should be able to pee in both the male and female toilet without any form of prejudice.

Xumgender – And last but certainly not least, we have a gender which according to the commandments of Tumblr is never truly satisfied with their gender and has to constantly change their identity just to feel some kind of value and self-worth. Funny as that sounds just like the other 99 whack jobs on this ridiculous list.

Knowing how to spot any one of the aforementioned gender identities had become not only a skill but a survival technique. And while I had no issue with people thinking that they were mythical beasts and genderless deities whilst living their lives in peace and harmony, I did have concerns with the militant approach that those on the left were aggressively pursuing in trying to get everyone to obey and act in accordance with their radical gender reform.

But as far as looking for a partner was concerned, I was looking for someone who only identified as one gender, and that gender was a man.

So, I ventured off into the formidable wilderness equipped with the knowledge of all 100 genders, and most importantly – the ability to overcome them in the event I inadvertently swiped right on a non-gendered androgyne who wanted to absorb my cis-gendered soul.

Even if I was desperate for a boyfriend, I didn't' want my soul mate to have gender non-conforming spirts spookily residing from within them. At this point in my life my dating life was scary enough as it was, without having to call an exorcist every time my nonconforming significant other ejaculated over my face.

CHAPTER 8

KNOCK DOWN GINGER

It was just another ordinary Tuesday evening when I proceeded to do the monotonous routine of checking Tinder – normally made up of illiterate fat old men who looked like they were child sex offenders, and African men claiming that I had inherited a million pound from a long distant great aunt somewhere in a remote village in Kenya. But in between profile pictures that looked like they were archived from Crime Watch, I noticed that a particularly handsome chap had messaged me in my inbox, and to top it off – wasn't an obvious looking spammer telling me to send over my bank details and passwords to all my social media accounts either.

Oliver was thirty years old and an administration assistant in Asda, a job in which he had been in for a remarkable fifteen years and considerably longer than any relationship that I had ever been in. I meticulously scanned his Tinder profile, looking for any sign of gender-fluidity or mention of his preferred pronouns that I had rigorously learnt from Tumblr to look out for, but to my surprise, all I could see was a generic dating bio that vaguely mentioned his interest in music, which was not particularly useful considering that most people liked listening to music.

Our first exchange of messages was pleasant and pretty conventional, especially considering that it was at this part in the conversation that I would normally find myself deleted and blocked into obscurity for having the 'controversial' opinion that British taxpayers shouldn't be forking out for prosthetic penises on the NHS. "Just to let you that I am a Trump fan," I prewarned Oliver in the event my political views could potentially set him off into an epileptic fit as it had done with Ronald previously.

Whilst I hated the fact that it had come down to having to give notice of my political stance before I had even met a date in person, at least I was preparing myself for the possibility of having to call emergency services if my date were suddenly to ignite in flames after finding out that I was a conservative. "So what?" was his surprising response back, as I breathed out a huge sigh of relief that Oliver seemingly wasn't another exasperating leftist with acute mental health issues.

After a few days of back and forth messaging, I also learnt that Oliver was fanatically obsessed with the high-kicking finger-pointing girl group, the Spice Girls. This was a huge relief, considering that I had so far been on a date with a non-binary shapeshifter who would later go on to become a transwoman, and an American national who hated being American, so going on a date with someone whose only notion of democracy was 'girl power' was rather refreshing.

We decided to meet near the Southbank area beside the River Thames, which had always been one of my favourite areas, along with its thriving bars, restaurants, and the infamous London Eye Ferris wheel, which I had still yet to ride. However, as luck would have it, I was currently suffering from the severe condition of man flu and felt like I was on the blink of death as I trudged on to meet my date – despite suffering from fatigue and a body temperature of 38C.

Arriving at Westminster Station, just across from the Palace of Westminster, I plodded past the mounted street performers decked up as living statues and feeling every bit the rusty sculpture myself as I made my way towards Westminster Bridge. The area was always brimming with people, mostly tourists – who franticly posed for Instagram photos alongside Westminster Bridge as if they had never seen or stepped foot on a bride before. And while the area of Westminster was packed with tourists posing for egocentric social media pictures, a few years ago, those conceited selfies were noticeably absent.

In 2017, six people were murdered and more than fifty people left injured by an Islamic terrorist who drove and mowed down innocent pedestrians who were simply going about their lives on what should have been just another mundane day in the city. However, it was Phillip Schofield who had truly inspired me in the aftermath of that tragedy when he heroically walked across the very same bridge the next day in a fearless display of courageousness that left me awestruck and lost in admiration as he posted his gallantness on social media for the world to see. So, walking across the very same bridge that the brave TV presenter and newly out of the broom cupboard homosexual gallantly minced across after such profound tragedy made me feel lionhearted, as I made my way to meet Oliver on what potentially could be another tragic date, or inadvertently strolling into the path of a crazed Jihadist ready to butcher me into a halal happy meal.

A whole thirty minutes had passed, and there was still no sign of Oliver in sight as I swiftly checked my phone while looking to see if I had received a message in letting me know that he was running late. Having coughed enough times to warrant a world record while wondering if I had been stood up, Oliver finally emerged through the mass of people that had descended upon the area, and to my utter surprise, there wasn't a dangling earring or pair of clanking high heels insight as he swiftly walked towards me. "Hey," smiled Oliver, as he greeted me with a delicate hug and the obligatory excuse for being half an hour late. "I'm so sorry I am late; someone threw themselves onto the tracks on the Central Line," Oliver claimed, as I continued to cough myself into extinction. While waiting a whole half an hour in London for a date to arrive was considered the epitome of rudeness, I couldn't exactly moan about Oliver turning up late, especially if someone had apparently committed suicide and inconveniently disrupted everyone's journey in the process. "Oh, that's awful!" I gasped, as I resonated with the deceased person currently frazzling on the track of the Northern Line.

Hastily putting my hand over my mouth as I coughed what felt like an erupting volcano in the back of my throat, we walked along the Southbank and towards a coffee shop as we made our way inside and perched upon two comfortable chairs conveniently positioned in the corner and away from the hordes of tourists that had assembled outside. "So, isn't Geri Halliwell a Tory?" I asked Oliver, as I sipped on my mocha while attempting to defuse the blistering apocalypse that was currently residing in my throat.

I always had a theory that Ginger Spice was, in fact, a fully-fledged Tory when she strutted on stage in her iconic Union Jack dress and had once declared that Margaret Thatcher was the 'original Spice Girl' in a magazine interview. The former grocer's daughter had seemingly inspired the young girl from Watford who would later go on to become one-fifth of the biggest selling girl band of all time, and while not publicly declaring her political persuasions, I could almost imagine Halliwell, who herself was half Spanish from a mum who migrated from a small village in

Spain, voting to leave the EU in the 2016 referendum. After all, having grown up in the UK and seeing first-hand the vast difference between hardworking migrants like her mother who migrated to the country legally before the freedom of movement of people was even a concept, to some EU nationals who in recent years unashamedly travelled to the UK for an all-expenses-paid trip courtesy of the British taxpayer – I figured that Geri was more likely to be Tory Spice than an advocate for uncontrolled mass migration, as I looked on towards the resident Spice Girls connoisseur to give me his opinion. "I dunno," shrugged Oliver, as he ploddingly took a bite from his sandwich. So much for stimulating conversation and intelligent dialogue, I thought to myself, as I gazed outside from where we were sitting while admiring the scene of blissfully engrossed couples strolling along with the backdrop of St. Paul's Cathedral – coughing myself into annihilation in the process.

Oliver wasn't that intellectual, witty or even remotely engaging as I murmured my way through a catalogue of topics that I thought would be good subject matter to discuss over on a first date. However, it was only when Oliver initiated the conversation on his terms, did he seemingly discover that he could talk. And when he discovered that ability – he wouldn't shut up. "Did you know that Geri was originally going to name her third album Disco Sister?" babbled Oliver, as he relayed upon me the unavailing piece of trivia as if he was imparting Winston Churchill's deathbed confessions.

We hadn't even established if Geri was a secret Tory, and yet Oliver had briskly moved on to the inner-workings of her solo career. I managed to give a vague look of interest and nod my head in acknowledgement as I internally cursed myself for leaving the warm sanctuary of my bed just so I could listen to useless clutter of Spice Girls information that would provide no purpose what so ever during the duration of my life.

After an hour of listening to Oliver waffle on about the philosophy of girl power, it was clear that we had absolutely nothing in common what so ever – the fact that my senses were progressively becoming worse since I was wheezing each time I took a breath didn't help save this fledging date either.

As I hideously coughed out my internal organs plagued with phlegm and bacteria, I just wanted to go home, take a few pills of paracetamol, and sleep forever. However, the lingering inner English adequate that had perched upon my shoulder was subconsciously preventing me from making my excuses and abruptly leaving, so instead, I continued to politely look engaged as if I was intellectually stimulated whilst Oliver continued to indoctrinate me with Spice Girls propaganda.

"I saw Spice World when it first came out on Boxing Day," recounted Oliver, as if watching a cheesy film on the day of its release was the equivalent of winning the Noble Peace Prize. "Oh really?" I spiritlessly replied, while at this point in the date wanting to do a Sporty Spice and high kick him into obscurity. I was bored and becoming increasingly irritated as I felt my nostrils itching to let out another enormous sneeze. But I soldiered on and kept calm with all the might and resistance of an Englishman in the trenches, despite my date being an absolute airhead with no redeeming qualities other than his tedious Spice Girls drivel.

Being the overly polite individual that I was, any sign of unleashing my inner Scary Spice anger was kept to a minimum and internalised from view, as we finally left the confines of the coffee shop and back amongst the legions of heedless tourists outside. We began to walk along the bustling Southbank as the sound of laughter from families on a day out filled the greying skies, whilst the same busking street performers smothered in sliver paint stood in silence while masquerading as statues desperate for a bit of loose change. While the atmosphere and vibrancy of the Southbank were always fun to be around – even for a melancholy Londoner who had seen it a thousand times before, I wished I had stayed in the warmth of my cosy bedlinen to hibernate and avoid all unnecessary social interactions with people, especially my intensely irritating date.

To say that this date was so far a waste of my time was an understatement, which so far had consisted of having song lyrics transcribed to me, to learning the shoe size of each Spice Girl in numerical order. By this point, I was probably looking sulkier and more miserable than Posh Spice being offered a full-fat buffet with extra calories. Say you'll be there? – at that moment in time, I wish I was anywhere but there.

It was during that moment of realisation that I was on a crap date that I should have done a Ginger Spice and made my excuses and done a runner, but alas there I was, silently nodding along with the bare minimum of enthusiasm as Oliver regurgitated yet more useless Spice Girls facts in my direction.

The irony was that I found Oliver quite attractive; he was handsome in an unconventional kind of way with his receding hairline and cockney accent that didn't sound like it belonged to an overbearing Spice Girls enthusiast. But with a lack of spark and feeling like I was deteriorating with each passing second, this was not the night when '2 would become 1' – on the contrary, it was the night that I would overdose on cough syrup and keel over. "You know that I met Geri, right?" Oliver excitedly revealed as I braced myself for the prospect of yet another extensive tale from the Spice Girls Scholar.

"I've met her about 22 times so far. She once accidentally spat in my face as she was talking to me. I didn't wash my face for a whole week after that," Oliver proudly beamed, as he smiled with contentment over having Geri Halliwell's dribble inadvertently hurled in his face. "No way!" I cringed, while also slyly trying to examine Oliver's face for any trace of Geri's salvia still festering on his face. "Yeah, she even follows me on Instagram, she knows who I am," bragged Oliver, as I still reeled from the disgust in finding out that Oliver had not washed his face for an entire week after being spat on by Geri Halliwell.

I wouldn't have been surprised at this point if Oliver had told me that Baby Spice had pulled down her pink frilly knickers and urinated on his face, as we continued strolling across the concreate paved walkway of the Southbank. But as I mentally prepared myself in trying not to look visibly disgusted if Oliver were actually to reveal that Emma Bunton had pissed on his face, he suddenly looked at me with the kind of revulsion that one would have if they accidentally found their parent's sex tape stashed away behind the sofa. "How can you stand there and judge me considering that you are a Trump fan?" snapped Oliver, as I looked on in stunned silence. And there it was... To be fair, it had only taken three hours of excruciating boredom in having the entire Spice Girls back-catalogue regurgitated back to me before Oliver's true colours were revealed – and they weren't exactly the 'colours of the world' either, as Oliver let slip his disdain for my political views.

We hadn't even gone on to covering Victoria Beckham's musical solo career yet (and to be honest, that wouldn't have taken a long time to dissect) before my political position was once again being criticised and condemned by someone from Tinder whose only accomplishment in life was having Geri Halliwell's gob spat in their face. "Wait, I thought you said you weren't interested in politics?" I pointed out, as I immediately stopped walking and turned to face Oliver. "I'm not, but everyone knows that he is a racist. Building a wall, locking kids in cages, that's racist, how can you condone that?" Oliver scolded as if he had now suddenly transformed from spice boy to CNN News Anchor in the blink of an eye. Normally I would have defended my political position with the poise and conviction of a Tory who had grown accustomed with moronic accusations of fascism and white supremacy, but as I let out another sneeze, the last thing I wanted to do was argue over politics with someone who probably thought that the second amendment was the name of a cocktail. "Well, it's been a lovely day, but it's getting late, and I should get back home now," I responded, as the feeling of itchiness tickled the back of my throat with another inevitable cough on the arising. "Oh..." gasped a shocked Oliver. "I hope I didn't offend you?" he consoled, as he looked at me with a concerned look on his face while probably realising that he had offended me. "No, not at all," I convincingly reassured him, as I proceeded to turn around and walk towards the direction of Waterloo Station.

"Message me when you get home," yelled Oliver through the crowds of tourists, as I walked further away from where I had left him standing. "Sure," I bellowed back while sounding like I had swallowed an entire lawnmower and gargled down a bottle of sawdust. I knew that I wouldn't message Oliver when I got home and would probably never see him again, as I trudged past the very same street performers still silently positioned in the same pose they were held in when I last walked past – all with only a fiver between them after a hard day's work.

I wondered how long they had silently posed for outside in the cold mimicking stiff sculptures for the amusement of disinterested tourists with barely enough to scrape together to top up their Oyster card, as I made my way into the warmth of Waterloo Station and down the familiar hallowed corridors of the London Underground. I boarded the tube and found myself a vacant seat on the Jubilee line which in itself was a rarity on a weekend as I perched myself down in between an older gentleman who looked like he had seen better days and a paunchy gothic-looking girl who just looked like she wanted to slit her wrists and die.

As the train joltingly made its way through the darkened narrow tunnels of the London Underground, I was able to find a free chair and gather my thoughts and digest exactly what had just happened.

Apart from demising from man flu and being on a boring date with a Spice Girls screwball, once again my political views had been decimated by someone who had probably never even been inside a polling booth before, let alone have the understanding and comprehension to even grasp what he had just accused me of being. While I had no objection at being challenged and even debating on a date, the fact of the matter was that when I was being implied as being an inherent racist for simply being a fan of the democratically elected President of the United States, it made me question how the subtle use of being labelled a racist for simply having a differing political view had ever become acceptable – especially as it cheapened the severity of actual racism by using the term loosely when it was not warranted.

After the mandatory routine of narrowly avoiding elbows and dodging oversized rucksacks on the tube, I finally managed to arrive back home, where Lena and Sofia were both in the front room and watching a film on Netflix. I hurried straight to the kitchen and proceeded to put three tablets of paracetamol in my mouth as I gargled down the medication with a glass of water before joining my flatmates in the front room.

It almost felt like déjà vu as I sat down on the sofa next to Lena and began to moan about my misadventures in Spice World, as Sofia silently listened from the other sofa across the room. "So, you left the date because he was a Spice Girls fan?" hissed Lena, as that familiar stern Polish gaze stared fixedly at me. "No!" I laughed, as I coughed for what seemed like the millionth time that day. "I left because he was another judgmental idiot who criticised me for being a Trump fan," I rebuked, as Lena continued looking at me with a frowned expression. "Oh my god, mate..." Lena sighed, looking at me like I had just been casually jogging through Gaza without a bulletproof vest. "Where do you meet these guys?" she jabbed while insinuating that maybe using Tinder wasn't exactly the best method in finding a boyfriend who didn't identify as a non-binary bowling ball or who wasn't politically intolerant. "Keep trying, George," replied Sofia in her softy spoken Spanish accent, as she demonstrated why she was always the more optimistic housemate compared to the unrelenting sternness of Lena. "Sometimes people meet their soulmate on the first date, while other times it may take twenty dates before you finally meet the one," reassured Sofia, as she gave me a firm smile and a nod of encouragement.

While I appreciated her moral support, I was still reeling from the after-effects of a string of bad dates and was already emotionally exhausted, so the prospect of another sixteen dates before I could potentially meet someone who didn't happen to be a far-left queer with a weird Spice Girls' fixation didn't exactly leave me feeling optimistic. As a homosexual man living in London, when it came to my options and methods of meeting other gay or bi-sexual men who were not over-sexualised deviants or strutting around thinking they were RuPaul, my choices were pretty much next to none. I had so far met a non-binary person who would later go on to become a transsexual woman and a spice boy who was salivating in Geri Halliwell's drool.

Feeling groggy and almost ready to pass out, I said goodnight to both Lena and Sofia and made my way to my bedroom as I got unchanged and crawled into my bed. But like most millennials who can't sleep before they go through the ritual of checking their phone, I checked my WhatsApp to see if Oliver had been online. I thought about the events of our date, and despite the fact he had been critical and attacked me for my political leanings, maybe I had been too hard on him.

As a Tory, I had become accustomed to being politically dissected for my political views, and if it wasn't for the fact that I had ten tons of phlegm legally occupying my respiratory system, I probably would have challenged him back and fought my ground. It had been a few hours since Oliver had told me to let him know that I was home, so the very least I could do was message him to let him know that I had not been viciously shanked by a 'roadman' walking through the darkened streets of the People's Republic of Hackney.

I went to message Oliver to let him know that I had got home safely only to see that I had been abruptly blocked. Instead of a photo of the Spice Girls that had previously been his display picture, all I could see now was that familiar grey silhouette which meant that I had been officially cancelled and ghosted just like all the other times before. The irony in being blocked by Oliver was that I wasn't one bit surprised, as I switched my phone on silent mode and laid my head on the plumpness of my cushion. Apart from it being casually implied that I was a racist for supporting President Trump, and learning that Geri Halliwell dribbles when she talks, the date with Oliver had been completely monotonous and uneventful, with more sexual chemistry between a Rabi and Jeremy Corbyn than there was between myself and the Spice Girls sage.

Maybe it was the fact that I was a Trump supporter that Oliver couldn't fathom, or maybe it was because I didn't respond enthusiastically enough overhearing the same wearisome Spice Girls gospel that made my date block me. But either way, I wasn't going to lose sleep over the fact that I had been abruptly ejected from Spice World, as I returned back to the real world of reality.

CHAPTER 9

BREXIT OR BOTTOM?

There have been many historical moments in the 4.543 billion years of earth. Everyone alive to witness it remembers where they were on July 1969 when Apollo 11 landed on the moon and Neil Armstrong first took those small steps and giant leaps into history. But while stepping foot onto the surface of the moon was truly a momentous occasion, no one single event in history has been as far-reaching and as impactful as that significant moment when Steve Bookstein was crowned the first-ever contestant to win the X-Factor. OK… maybe scrap that one. But another major event that I remember vividly was on June 2016 when the UK voted to leave the European Union in the largest exercise of democracy in Britain's long democratic history.

I also remember what I was doing when I found out that we were handing in our P45 to the European Union – my head was firmly positioned down my mum's kitchen sink as I violently regurgitated everything but my intestines. On what should have been a celebratory occasion in what Nigel Farage had triumphantly dubbed the UK's 'Independence Day' was instead spent savagery heaving while starring directly into my mum's kitchen sink after reeling from the aftermath of food poisoning from eating a dodgy kebab. But in between the intense vomiting and sounding like I was being strangled, it was reassuring to waking up to the news that 17.4 million Brits had voted to become independent and leave the European Union once and for all.

Brexit was also cathartic for me, as not only had I left one volatile and unhealthy relationship that day, but a day before, I also summoned up the courage to end another harmful and damaging relationship – this time with a long term boyfriend who had made me feel as inadequate and insufficient as being a reluctant member of a globalist elitist institution.

I first met Joe when I was twenty-six years old. He was younger than me at nineteen years old but seemed a lot more mature than his age led to believe. He had an adoring babyface but regularly worked out in the gym so had the body of a brawny and towering rugby player. Joe had dark brown hair with matching brown eyes and was often understated in the fashion department, wearing tracksuits and decked in his reliable Adidas trainers wedged on his mammoth size twelve feet.

I had just received my political economics degree in University a month prior but found myself working for a local lawyer's firm gaining experience as a Social Media Assistant, where I was paid approximately £7.70 an hour to tweet and post photos on the firm's social media accounts. How I got from studying political economics to getting paid to post photos on Facebook was anyone's guess, but it was a job and helped me pay the remaining balance of my student fee – which surprisingly had not been overindulged on cheap booze and student nights out.

Joe, on the other hand, had dropped out of sixth-form altogether and had got himself an apprenticeship in a local plumbing firm that his uncle conveniently owned. Joe was what they call in gay lingo 'straight-acting', meaning that if you met Joe down the pub on a Friday night, you wouldn't automatically assume that he was a prancing queen based solely on his sexuality. We met on Grindr, a notorious gay hook-up app in which 10% of blossoming homosexual relationships first come into fruition, with the other 90% being merely casual anal penetration in some damp park public toilet in the early hours of the morning.

Just like our means of meeting, our first date left a lot to be desired and lacked the romance and mystique that I had environed a first date to encompass. He was a broke teenager, and I was a Social Media Assistant still desperately paying off my student debt, but I had somehow managed to scrape a few pounds together which meant that we ended up in the picturesque surroundings of the local McDonalds branch. Joe wasn't political at all, which was great because he didn't know the difference between a Tory and a tomato, which made being a conservative in a relationship that much easier. "Fuck politicians, they are all the fucking same!" was often a sentence I would hear from a disgruntled Joe, whilst I excitedly waffled on about the latest political shenanigans that were occurring in Westminster. Joe was seemingly more interested in football and video games than the economy or foreign affairs, which apart from occasionally playing the odd game of Call of Duty here and there, I had no real interest in what so ever – let alone getting my head around the technicalities of the offside rule in a football match.

So, I and Joe had absolutely nothing in common, we couldn't muster up ten pounds between us to even afford a hamburger, and Joe's idea of a romantic night out was at the local McDonalds which was loitered with homeless people hallucinating on crack while unflinchingly injecting themselves inside the disabled toilets.

To say that our relationship was mindlessly juvenile was an understatement, yet, despite the disenchanting surroundings, we strangely fell for each other.

Joe officially became my first ever boyfriend at the grand age of twenty-six after asking me out as he waited with me by the bus stop on a chilly evening in February. We spent a great deal of time together in the coming months, often living in one another's pocket as we idly vegetated in my bedroom while also becoming emotionally reliant on one another to the point where it soon became unhealthy. "I don't know how I put up with you," Joe would abruptly sneer, as he looked over at me while I was blissfully preoccupied reading political literature as he laid spread out on my bed seemingly bored and resentful that I was not giving him the attention that he craved.

That's where the name-calling first began. At first, it was crude comments over my political interests, which he never truly understood, to then going on to insinuating that he was the best thing that had ever happened to me. Joe would often threaten that if I left him, nobody else would want me, as the psychological torment of being made to feel inadequate continued as the weeks progressed. And it could occur at the most casual of times – cuddling up together on my bed at my parents' house before Joe suddenly announcing that nobody could replace him if I decided to end the relationship, as I looked on in perplexment.

Repeatedly being told that I was a nuisance to be around while at the same time hearing that my life was not worth living outside of the toxic relationship that I had inadvertently found myself in, and I was pretty much in the same dilemma that many Brexiteers found themselves in when it was time to tick the ballot box on the day of the referendum. While comparing my psychologically controlling and exasperated ex-boyfriend to a political and economic union of European member states may seem a bit farfetched, comparing EU membership to a disdainful and emotionally unhinged teenager wasn't that far off.

Here we had the European Union; a bunch of unelected bureaucrat bullies whose contempt towards the UK and those who dared to defy the divine rule of Brussels was as comparable to any emotionally abusive relationship that I had ever been in. And while my ex-boyfriend may not have been a bumbling drunkard like the former European Commission president Jean-Claude Juncker – whose anti-Brexit ramblings were the kind of thing you would hear down at the local alcoholics anonymous, at least Juncker was transparent in his detestation for British democracy after we had executed our democratic right to vote to leave the European Union – with Joe it was a lot more manipulative and cunning.

The putdowns were always much more indirect but also maliciously coordinated, something which the European Union were never great at hiding. I had got used to being treated with such mockery and denigration from Joe that it had become the norm. Just like the normality of being raised as a citizen in the European Union in which uncontrolled and limitless number of migrants entering the country was as ordinary as waiting months for an appointment to see my local GP – it was just something that I had just gotten used to, despite it affecting me negatively.

I had gotten used to walking around town until the early hours with Joe doing absolutely nothing, as he begged me to lend him more money on outstanding debts. We never did anything exciting or remotely romantic and would instead just spend days routinely in Joe's house, where he lived with his mum and younger sister, as we binge-watched entire series on Netflix while ordering take away food, which I always ended up paying for. Joe's dad had abruptly left the family when he was five years old, moving to Manchester to live with another woman and would later go on to give birth to three more children, none of which Joe had ever met or seen. Joe's father would occasionally travel down to London to see him on birthdays, but, for the most part, their relationship was as empty and meaningless as a Diane Abbott mathematical class. Maybe that's why Joe was so forceful and aggressive I would often ponder, as the lingering effects of an absent father turned an aimless son into an authoritarian psychopath.

The barrage of excuses from Joe, who never had any money to pay his mum some housekeeping or even afford to pay his half of a meal, always meant that I was expected to dig deep into my pockets and loan him even more money – money which as a then broke and severely penniless Social Media Assistant, I just did not have. It was times like this that I seriously thought about becoming a socialist and milking that indefinite anti-capitalist cash cow that magically grew on trees. But even though I was a broke and impressionable severely in debt student, I still believed that hard work and perseverance always paid off rather than relying on government handouts to provide for my terrible eating habits.

The tempting allure of free things failed to entice me as I continued to hone my craft and work extra hard in my job, as I skipped the obligatory University student day out to Glastonbury, which meant that I was immune from Labour Party subliminal messaging while plodding around knee-deep in cow manure and communism propaganda. But away from work, my sadomasochist relationship with Joe continued – just like the relationship between a Remainer and the European Union. And although I was never psychologically spanked by Juncker and his floppy croissant, I had become emotionally reliant in a disparaging relationship with Joe and the EU where I had become passively subservient to a psychological abuser who constantly inflicted pain and humiliation towards me.

It was as if Joe derived pleasure from me experiencing pain, and that by making me feel subservient towards him, he knew that

I would never leave him no matter what he said or done. But then Brexit happened, and everything changed for the better. After winning re-election in May 2015, then Conservative Prime Minister David Cameron announced that there would be a national referendum after pressure from Nigel Farage and the UKIP Party, in which UK citizens would get to decide if the UK would leave or remain in the European Union. Finally, after years of trade restrictions, uncontrolled free movement of people, and having the volume level in my headphones dictated to by unelected bureaucrats in Brussels, I was finally going to experience life in an independent and self-governing nation.

Brexit and the promise of a prosperous future in which the UK would become independent once again and start making our own decisions as a self-governing democracy was the wake-up call and realisation that I needed that Joe was my Junker and that he just had to go.

The announcement of a referendum sent the biased pro-EU media channels like the BBC and Channel 4 into a frenzied panic of cataclysm predictions and doomed visions of the UK becoming some kind of post-apocalyptic ravaged wasteland, as the looming presence of project fear put trepidation into the hearts of British voters. And while many were preparing for the apocalypse and hysterically building nuclear bunkers in their back gardens over the reality that the UK could vote to leave the EU, I was contemplating on how to end things with Joe.

Unluckily for me, I was at university during the height of Brexit when the referendum campaign was in full gear where the hostility and alienation of being a Brexiteer in an insanely leftist university were so intense, that even using the toilet was seen as a form of cultural appropriation against European migrants.

My political economics class was a lesson in wokeness, and every day I discovered a new way of how to offend someone. I was a vocal Brexiteer and had made my intentions publicly known that I would be voting to leave the European Union. Our lecturer, who was supposed to be teaching us the social science of production and trade, instead spent thirty minutes lecturing me about my apparent 'white male privilege' and how my biological skin tone had genetically engineered my decision to vote to leave the European Union. I argued that the reasons behind me using my democratic vote to leave the European Union were purely based on national sovereignty and economics and trade, something which I found ironic having to justify and explain considering that I was literally in a political economics class. But alas, according to my forty-five-year-old Caucasian and female political economics lecturer, who had the most bizarre pink and green dyed hair that I had ever seen, it was my so-called 'whiteness' that had unconsciously made me decide to vote to leave the EU – not the fact that I wanted to remove power from unelected officials from Brussels who lacked any form of democratic accountability.

If I was looking for some kind of moral support from my classmates against the pink and green behemoth casually labelling me a racist in front of everyone for simply having a differing political opinion, then I had come to the wrong class.

Sadly, many of my classmates were unrelenting Remainers who cared very little for the reasoning behind my decision in wanting to leave the European Union, let alone being tolerant enough to hear my rationale for wanting to use my democratic vote in a way that perhaps did not conform to their own.

Brexit had turned what once was a rational and logical political debate between opposing views into a full-scale war, and places like my political economics class had become the battlefield. Just the mere mention of Brexit in passing conversation in the university halls would turn sound-minded and supposedly intellectual people into mentally unbalanced ravaging monsters.

My university was hallowed pro-EU ground and so I found myself anxiously avoiding all forms of contact, as just an accidental passing glance with a Remainer could have severe consequences and end with my annihilated corpse being ripped apart by the sharpened fangs of Remainer cannibals out for Brexit blood.

The patriotic stench oozed from my trembling body as I dashed from my political economics class straight to the safe confines of my dormitory in which I made sure my locks were bolted tight.

Project fear and the intense apprehension of the UK leaving the European Union had turned Remainers, the very same type of middle class, avocado-eating hipsters who for so long had advocated for tolerance and a gentler kind of politics, into demonic creatures who had descended into absolute madness and intolerance. I would restlessly lay awake in my dorm room late at night and hear the faint sound of scratching fingertips crawling on my dormitory door as if I had hastily barricaded myself in like I was in the middle of a pending zombie apocalypse. But instead of being in a scene straight out of a Night of The Living Dead, I found myself unintentionally in the middle of a political storm in which the UK was about to make its most important decision that would go on to affect the political landscape for generations to come.

On the day that it was announced that the UK had voted to leave the European Union, I woke up feeling a sense of patriotism, exuberance and glee, and with a Facebook friend list full of resentful Remainers noticeably absent from my social media account. I had also reached the comprehension that my boyfriend was just another indolent sperm of Generation Z expecting an entitled freebie, and that my conservative values and future happiness were being compromised for the sake of a predestined relationship that would only end up on a council estate and reliant on Universal Credit for the rest of our lives. With a splitting headache and the remains of the previous night's kebab literally about to spew up from my throat, I hastily rushed downstairs and shoved my mum out of the way as I disgorged the remains of the undercooked meat down the kitchen sink.

My mum was watching BBC Breakfast on the TV in the kitchen as I vaguely made out the sound of despairing disappointment in the presenter's tone as they relayed the news that 52% of the UK had voted to leave the European Union. While I celebrated the UK voting to leave the EU with my head imbedded down my mum's kitchen sink, it also dawned on me that I had something else to celebrate too as I had just recently become single after ending things with Joe over WhatsApp the night before.

For me, it came to a head when Joe kicked up a fuss about me wanting to go out on a Brexit eve pub crawl with a few thinly dispersed Brexiteer friends from University and drown our depended misery, adamantly convincing ourselves that the prophecy of project fear would come to light and that the UK would overwhelmingly vote to remain in the EU.

Joe was uncompromising in that I not go out to commiserate with my fellow Brexiteers but instead spend the night with him in yet another Netflix marathon while I ordered us the usual deep-pan Margherita pizza from UberEATS. "You're cheating on me init!" snapped Joe on the phone, as I told him that feeling pity over remaining in the EU was more important than another night of Netflix and chill.

This was the umpteenth time that I had been accused of cheating on Joe within the last month – losing count over the number of times that I was charged with the crime of having sordid affairs with everyone from the Pakistani shop keeper, to my biological cousin. And while in some cultures procreating with family members may be the norm, I was not going to indulge in the activity of keeping it in the family anytime soon, especially when most of my cousins looked like they had been hit in the face with a shovel.

To assure an increasingly paranoid Joe that I was not the local neighbourhood whore, I was reluctantly forced to show him every form of digital communication that I had ever sent out or received. Everything had to be checked over and inspected until he was certain that I was not shagging anyone with a penis and a pulse. With such scrutiny and intense analysis placed over me, I couldn't even imagine that even Hillary Clinton had to face such dissection when handling over her 30,000 classified emails to the FBI. But yet here I was, being made to go through all my messages by my jealous and insecure teenage boyfriend like I was on trial and being investigated by a federal judge.

The irony in being vehemently accused of cheating was that I was convinced that Joe was cheating on me. Like most suspecting millennials void of any face to face communication skills, I decided to confront Joe on WhatsApp with my suspicion that he was cheating on me with evidence of screenshots that I had taken of his questionable social media activity from comments he had left men on Instagram. "Are you cheating on me?" I wrote on WhatsApp, as I anxiously waited for the two pending ticks to change to blue, indicating that he had read and received my message. A few minutes later and I had seen that he had read the message as I rapidly-paced myself up and down my bedroom.

I waited with bated breath to receive a notification from my phone and a response from Joe, but instead of being bombard with excuses, I simply received a resounding "Yes" as I checked my phone to see his response.

At this stage, I didn't have the energy nor the regard to ask him why he was cheating on me, or how long it had been going on for. I didn't even care as to who the main culprit could be in the line-up of Instagram suspects that he had seemingly been rendezvousing with behind my back. I think I was secretly relieved that I had finally found an escape route out of this toxic relationship – pondering over the times in which I had been made to feel inferior from a person who couldn't even remain faithful to me.

Rather than message him back with a long paragraph of reasons why I loathed him, I simply typed "Cool. Have a good life" before pressing the send button on my phone. While it certainly lacked the Shakespearean masterly and the poetic elegance of Romeo and Juliet – nevertheless, it was straight to the point, as I waited to see that he had received and read the message before promptly blocking him on WhatsApp and deleting his number from my phone. I never heard from Joe again after that final message had been sent, as I looked optimistically towards the future at the prospect of the UK negotiating future trading deals from outside of the European Union.

However, just like Brexit, my dating life would face indefinite delays to the point of frustration and despair, as I would later find out when I hopelessly tried to leave the single market myself.

CHAPTER 10

GREEN NEW ROMANCE

According to U.S. Representative and socialist poster girl Alexandria Ocasio-Cortez, we had twelve years left until the world would come to a blistering end due to climate change. This rather unnecessary predicament left me with twelve years to find a boyfriend, get married, and get a mortgage before we all deteriorated into volcanic ash. So, with the prospect of a global warming cataclysm and the lingering possibility of surviving on rations in a post-Brexit Britain, I was on borrowed time in finding love and settling down before I ended up dying alone and being eaten by radioactive cannibals.

Desperate times called for desperate matters, and so I did what any rational homosexual man who was looking for romance and commitment would do – I downloaded Grindr. Grindr, the most corrupt, immoral, sordid, and downright sleazy digital cesspit in the history of dating apps. Grindr was pretty much Tinder's queer and overly sexualised slutty cousin who seemingly had great difficulty in keeping their legs closed for a considerable amount of time. The landscape of Grindr pretty much consisted of penises, lots of penises actually, all being poked and plodded into some indiscriminate hole as users messaged whoever was within proximity for a convenient quick shag.

This was pretty much Grindr in a nutshell, and now I had ventured into its sordid planes looking for my prince charming. Maybe sweltering in the blistering heat of climate change and dying alone would be a better option, I pondered, as I browsed through the array of profiles of shirtless men and photos of enlarged bulges in briefs intensely poking back at me.

Grindr was quite literally a multi-coloured rainbow influx of testosterone and sexually transmitted disease and was everything that was disreputable with the homosexual lifestyle, as I took one firm swipe on my phone and, in an instant, had before my eyes every questionable and dodgy character within walking distance of the People's Republic of Hackney, and they weren't exactly the most enticing of options. There was the local 'aspiring rapper' who had downloaded Grindr on the down-low for a bit of discreet rectum probing in-between their drug trafficking shift down the end of the road. And then, there was the obligatory horny Eastern Europe Uber Driver who just wanted to snort drugs and spank me amid hallucinated ecstasy in the back of his car. And while there was a certain feeling of weird curiosity over the thought of having embedded handprints on my buttocks by a Romanian migrant, at this stage in my life, I just wanted the simple life and didn't particularly want semen squirted in my eyes as I laid stark naked in the back of a car.

I wasn't looking to discreetly suck off a married man behind the Job Centre, and I certainly didn't want to tuck my testicles into a pair of Primark frilly knickers just so I could experience a straight man with a kink for trannies on top of me either. So, it came as a complete shock when I received the infamous Grindr notification from my phone to signal that I had received a new message from someone who wasn't a sexaholic, commitment-phobic pervert with a fetish for stockings and strangulation.

Harry was twenty-two and was a biology student who lived in Islington in North London. Islington just so happened to be the mating ground of every cork-popping champagne socialist who loudly advocated for 'cultural enrichment' and open borders while never actually having crossed paths with a single refugee in their entire lives. But while the geography of Harry and where he lived left a lot to be desired, I certainly didn't want to judge the merits of a potential boyfriend based on the fact they resided in Jeremy Corbyn territory.

Harry only had two photos on his Grindr account, both of which he was wearing clothes and his private parts were not on full display for the entire world to see. Based on the fact that I had not yet seen his genitalia and that he had not asked me what my preference was in the bedroom department meant that after a few generic WhatsApp messages, I decided to ask him out on a date. At this point, I figured that he was not a distorted sex-crazed deviant and was relatively good-looking, and after my last few dates, I figured that the chances of meeting another non-binary person who ticked the infinity box on the gender spectrum, or the probability of encountering another angry leftist who got triggered into a frenzied rage over Trump killing terrorists in Iran was proportionately quite small. So, deciding to meet Harry outside Leicester Square station on a Saturday afternoon, I was neither anxious nor concerned that a cross-dressing member of Antifa reeling of cat urine would show up to greet me.

In fact, so relaxed I was that this date would not involve my political positions being ripped to shreds and hung to dry like a pair of Bill Clinton's soiled underwear, I casually ventured into the

Burger King that was across the road from the station and ordered myself a chicken burger with medium-sized Pepsi while perched on a table and chair opposite the window overlooking Leicester Square so I could see when Harry eventually arrived.

I had arrived eighteen minutes before our scheduled time and was feeling slightly peckish so had plenty of time to indulge in processed fast food while enjoying the seductive and addictive taste of carbohydrates, added sugar, and unhealthy fat as I tucked into my succulent chicken slain burger. As I polished off the last remaining crisp coating of the chicken that was firmly in my mouth, my phone frantically began to vibrate as an unknown number flashed before my phone screen.

I was always pretty hesitant in answering anonymous calls as it always ended up being an unscrupulous Indian call centre trying to claim that I had lost a limb or a finger in some devastating car accident and that I urgently needed to purchase some kind of health insurance plan from somewhere in Mumbai for my limbs to miraculously grow back.

Swallowing the last piece of food circulating in my mouth and taking a sip of the drink, I hesitantly answered my phone. "Hello?" I answered, while half expecting a foreign accent to reply instantly wanting my sort code and PIN. "Hey," replied an English sounding accent that didn't sound like they wanted to scam me for my inheritance money. "Are you in Burger King by any chance?" asked the mysterious unknown caller as I suspiciously began to carefully scan my surroundings while looking to see if I was being watched by some kind of secret intelligence agent.

"Who is this?" I asked the unknown caller, now slightly frightened that all those times that I had tweeted unfavourably about Hillary Clinton were about to come back and haunt me. "It's me, Harry," laughed the caller, as I breathed a huge sigh of relief that I was not about to mysteriously give up the ghost-like Jeffrey

Epstein. "I'm here," revealed Harry, as I looked out the window opposite me to notice a man resembling what I assumed Harry to look like smiling and waving at me.

Cute, I thought, as I waved back with a smile. Harry was not what I was expecting as I took my tray and empty rubbish before dropping it in the bin beside my table. He was good-looking and pleasantly normal. In fact, from what I could see, there didn't seem to be dangling chain earring or Spice Girls t-shirt insight.

On the contrary, he was decked out in a smart pair of black trousers, complete with a white buttoned shirt and a brown trench coat, and looked every bit the elegant gentlemen and not the kind of person you would expect to be downloading a corrupt gutter app like Grindr. As I made my way out of Burger King and walked towards him, Harry reached out both of his arms and proceeded to embrace me with a hug as I reciprocated with a slightly awkward variation. "Nice to meet you," gushed Harry, still with a huge smile on his face as his dark blue eyes assuredly gazed at my nervous demeanour. "Lovely to meet you too," I replied, as I suddenly felt myself being overcome by a timorous shyness.

I couldn't explain why I had all of a sudden become timid as it was only a few moments ago that I was confidently devouring greasy food. And now here I was, trembling before a handsome young man smiling back at me. And then it dawned on me, I was nervous because I found Harry extremely attractive. Maybe it was his blonde flowing mane of hair brushed back into a neat parting or the fact that it was pretty obvious that he frequented the gym once or twice by the way his chest pushed out of his tightly buttoned shirt as if he was Clark Kent about to metamorphose into Superman.

But either way, Harry was extremely handsome, and I had not found someone this physically captivating since Ronald, the same Ronald who had formerly declared that my political perspective meant that I was not worthy to be loved before stomping off in a furore. "Do you want to grab a drink?" suggested Harry, as I desperately tried to grabble with my nerves. "That sounds good," I swiftly replied, while trying my best to look as cool as a cucumber. From Leicester Square we walked a few blocks though the mass of untamed tourists towards Trafalgar Square where Harry had recommended that we go to a pompous rooftop bar overlooking the city that he had previously been to before.

The Volary Bar was situated right across from Nelson's Column and was the perfect ambience for a first date as I sipped on delicate cocktails while passionately engrossed in tantalising conversation all while under the patriotic glare of Lord Nelson. First dates couldn't get much better than this as I raised my glass of daiquiri and toasted Harry who firmly held a glass of dry martini as he flashed that alluring smile that had made me turn into a bashful nincompoop. "So how long have you been single for?" I asked Harry, while also systematically breaking one of the three subjects that first dating lore forbid us to ask. "I've never really had a boyfriend, to tell you the truth," Harry revealed, as he took a light sip of his drink. "So, I'm quite eager to experience love," he continued, before putting down his glass and proceeding to give me a cheeky wink from across the table. But before I could respond in kind to the suggestive signal of affection from Harry, we were both suddenly startled by the blaring sound of muffled noise and what sounded like someone talking loudly on a megaphone from outside of the bar.

Perplexed, we gave one another a look of confusion as to what the raucous noise could be, as we both left our table and made our way towards the balcony where it also seemed that other curious guests had come to assemble and investigate what the commotion was as we looked over the edge of the balcony which overlooked Trafalgar Square to see what looked like thousands of people congregating near Nelson's Column.

People were holding banners and waving placards in the air while simultaneously chanting together as if they were in the midst of some kind of social demonstration. As we were situated high on the rooftop and quite far up from the ever-growing crowd, we were not able to make out what exactly people were chanting, or the reason why a large mass of people had suddenly descended upon Trafalgar Square. "Do you want to go down and see what is happening?" I asked Harry, who looked as every bit as curious as I did. "Sure, why not?" replied Harry, as we walked back to our table to grab our coats and make our way out of the bar. We made our way towards the lift as a group of customers made their way out of the doors as Harry signalled that I should enter the lift first once the group had walked past us.

Harry was intensely good-looking, charming, and an absolute gentleman, I happily thought to myself, as we both entered the lift and pushed the ground floor button to make our way down. While in the lift on the way down to the ground floor, I took the moment of solitude to return the compliment of the suggestive wink Harry had given me earlier across from the table.

Maybe the effects of the daiquiri had started to kick-in, or maybe it was the harmonising sound of the generic instrumental elevator music, but a sudden surge of energy suddenly came over my body and, without hesitation, I placed my lips on Harry's lips and proceeded to kiss him. This could have been a textbook '#MeToo' unwanted sexual contact moment, but, thankfully for me, my object of desire reciprocated my instantaneous smooch, and we both ended up kissing one another until the lift reached the ground floor.

"Well, that was certainly enjoyable," proclaimed Harry, as the lift announced that we had reached our floor – slowly pulling away from one another and out of our affectionate grip. "Yes… it was," I giggled, as we both hastily adjusted ourselves in an attempt not to look like we had just been snogging over seven levels of floors as we made our way out of the lift and outside of the building. As we both walked out onto the street and made our way towards Trafalgar Square, we were instantly met with the deafening sound of police sirens and car horns rapidly blaring in frustration – gazing upon what could only be best described as a scene resembling the chaotic and disorderly motion of an apocalypse in motion.

Trafalgar Square and the roads around it had been descended upon by what seemed like thousands of people, as angry motorists sat dormant in their vehicles and remained paralysed on the road. People were holding signs above their head that read 'Act now' while others were manically blowing through whistles whilst antagonistically waving their clinched fists high up into the air. "What the hell is happening?" I asked Harry completely baffled while looking around with a perplexed look on my face at the hordes of people prowling towards Nelson's Column. "I think this is Extinction Rebellion," replied Harry, as more people appeared seemingly out of nowhere and joined the ever-expanding herd that was taking shape.

"What is Extinction Rebellion?" I casually asked Harry, while still bewildered at the catastrophic scene that was happening around us. "You don't know about the dangers of climate change?" sneered Harry, now looking at me as if I had just passed carbon monoxide out of my backside. Extinction Rebellion was an environmental activist organisation made up of overwhelmingly white middle-class left-wing activists which would make even Jon Snow gasp in astonishment with the obscene amount of whiteness assembled in one place, who along with Hollywood millionaire actors and politicians, sermonized about the end of the world and how we were all responsible for contributing to an impending global environmental cataclysm that would eventually kill us all if we didn't quickly act and angrily protest on the streets.

In promoting climate change and apparent ecological collapse, Extinction Rebellion activists strenuously participated in mass civil disobedience by disrupting ordinary people's journey to work by supergluing themselves onto trains and roads in scenes that resembled the Woodstock Festival on steroids. It was a chaotic scene as nose ringed pagans and self-indulgent degenerate hippies set up camp and danced around to repetitive techno music, as clearly vexed motorists desperately struggled to find alternative routes to get home amid the climate carnage that Extinction Rebellion had created. And as angry black cab drivers ferociously screamed from the top of their lung's whilst bearded globe-trotting university graduates perched on yoga mats in the middle of the road, I could see why these environmental luvvies caused so much anger and resentment from everyday people.

I always found it annoyingly condescending when the likes of the Duke of Sussex and his narcissistic and conceited wife Meghan Markle vehemently preached to the masses at how we should all do our best to minimize and reduce our carbon footprint, while at the same time flying halfway around the world comfortably onboard gas-guzzling private planes just to splash out by the poolside with Elton John. So, when Harry asked the question of my understanding of climate change, I simply shrugged my shoulders.

Harry, who was still looking at me with complete disbelief, proceeded to yell at me over the noise of the crowd, "All life is going to come to an end unless we do something about it!" he shouted, as the pupils in his eyes began to evolve to a fiery red as if environmental doom was on the horizon. I didn't know if it was the atmosphere of the protest or if my lack of persuasion on climate change had offended Harry, but I certainly began to notice a slight change in the demeanour of the person who just a few moments ago I was canoodling within a lift. Harry had gone from having his tongue down my throat to now lecturing me of the apparent extreme weather effects and the breakdown of society that could occur because of climate change, as I simply noodled along and tried my best to look interested. As we made our way through the disorderly mob of people who all looked like they were hallucinating pink elephants, I began to feel like I was more on a crash course in global warming than a romantic first date. While I admired Harry's passion, the truth of the matter was that I didn't buy into the whole end of the world climate change crap that the likes of Leonardo DiCaprio condescendingly fearmongered to the public, as he sailed the seven seas on luxury yachts while sipping on crystal champagne from the waxed crotch of some younger Brazilian model that had inadvertently slid into his DM's on Instagram.

If Oprah Winfrey wasn't going to convince me that monstrous farting cows would bring about the end of the world, then Harry from Grindr certainly wasn't, as we continued walking through the hordes of dirty-looking hippies who looked like they hadn't seen a bath or an honest day's work in years. Harry continued to integrate me as if I had just been caught excreting a mass amount of plastic into the ocean. "How often do you recycle?" he quizzed, as I desperately tried to avoid being rampantly barged into by the obscene amount of pink-haired eco-warriors that were continuously forming around us like a horde of crawling zombies on weed. "I don't," I confessed to Harry, as we coincidentally passed a diesel-powered generator that Extinction Rebellion had brought along to the protest to power up one of their tents, which had been erected in the middle of the road.

"I can't believe that you don't recycle," snapped Harry, as he promptly covered his mouth to stop the sinister planet-destroying diesel fuel from entering his lungs – aggressively pumping from the generator that his Extinction Rebellion friends had dragged along with them. "To be honest, I think all of these protesters are virtue-signalling hypocrites," I rebuked, as we narrowly walked past the line of frustrated motorists stuck in traffic – incapable of movement as twerking protesters continued to block their path with their environmentally friendly wiggling bum cheeks.

"I mean, we've just walked past a diesel spewing generator for crying out loud," I continued, as the lingering stench of processed greasy food loitered in the air, with the sight of flabby environmental activists rapidly devouring their capitalistic Big Mac's further proving my point that this movement was nothing more than a virtue-signalling love fest.

Not wanting to acknowledge the dishonest displays of deceitfulness that was occurring around us, Harry merely gave me a look of disapproval, indicating that he was not best pleased with my sceptical attitude towards these so-called nature-loving eco-activists that he valued so much.

Fed up with being reprimand over not recycling and desperately wanting to rekindle the spark that had been beginning to develop before Extinction Rebellion proceeded to dump a mass of organic manure over my chances of finding love, I suggested to Harry that we leave the anti-capitalist anarchism of Trafalgar Square and go and find a nice quiet bar somewhere, preferably a place where we could have a nice drink without being told that the world was going to end.

We managed to catch a tube that had not been superglued by eco-activist millennials and made our way to Kings Cross, a part of London where the only green deals taking place were between the resident prostitutes and their pimps, as we ventured to a local bar just outside of the tube station.

However, my strategy to take Harry away from the impressionable grip of tree-hugging eco-nuts had not gone according to plan, and instead of lustfully winking at me as he had previously done, I was faced with a soured expression sitting across from the table, as Harry continued to scold me over my lack of environmental resources management. "We have a decade to save the planet before we all die," proclaimed Harry in a blood-curdling tone, as I blankly looked on while drinking my environmentally unfriendly pisco sour cocktail.

While I appreciated that Harry meant well in his one-man crusade to save us all from being burnt to a crisp like chlorinated chicken, I couldn't help but notice the rank hypocrisy in his campaign to get me to cut all meat intake and recycle everything in sight, as I pointed out his obvious double standards. "But you didn't have a problem with me eating processed meat from Burger King earlier?" I reminded him, as Harry looked on as vacantly as Greta Thunberg doing an organic poop on a composting toilet. "Well, who am I to judge?" shrugged Harry, as I looked at him with stern scepticism. "But that's the thing, you've been judging me since I told you that I don't recycle," I firmly pointed out, as Harry proceeded to take out his phone from out of his pocket and completely disregard what I had just said.

"Why are you currently guzzling and burning up the atmosphere with your iPhone and not talking to me?" I sneered, as Harry continued to swipe on his battery-powered manufactured phone without acknowledging a word that I was saying.

I was being deliberately ignored by Harry as he continued to look down at his phone, and if there was one thing that I despised more than being ghosted, it was purposely being given the cold shoulder when I was sitting right from across the table.

Maybe Harry was feeling stupid and had finally registered that he was not Captain Planet, but instead was just as hypocritical as everybody else in his self-righteous crusade to save humanity from impending doom. I took another swig of my drink and laid back into my chair before Harry suddenly stopped swiping on his phone and immediately lifted himself out of his chair. "I think I'm going to go now," Harry mumbled, as I sat up from my slumped position with a dumbfounded expression on my face. "Have I offended you?" I briskly replied, as I finally locked eyes with Harry after being disregarded by him while he was fiddling away on his phone. "I know I'm not perfect, but at least I'm doing my best to prevent climate change, which is more than I can say about you," sneered Harry – looking at me disdainfully as if I had just skinned a polar bear alive. It seems in pointing out the hypocrisy of Extinction Rebellion and Harry's own excessively conceited view of himself and his environmentalism – I had dented his ego.

I stayed firmly in my chair as I gazed upon Harry making his way through the entrance of the bar as a trail of fossil fuel lingered behind him. After the escapades of Ronald and Oliver and being lampooned over my political standings, I certainly was not going to dramatically run after somebody who got overly heated because I didn't recycle. I peered through the window from where I was sitting and could vaguely make out Harry at the end of the road, examining his phone.

Maybe he was in the process of blocking me, or maybe he was in the midst of an intellectual conversation with an anonymous headless torso on Grindr about the effects of greenhouse gas emissions, but either way, I didn't care, and in that instant, I took my phone from out of my coat pocket. If I was going to preserve the planet, the best place to start was by getting rid of useless clutter that I didn't need, so in an instant swipe – I deleted Grindr.

CHAPTER 11

WITHERING HEIGHTS

Call me old fashioned or maybe even slightly deluded, but I truly believed that monogamy and romance still existed, even in London where being ghosted was as bad of a trait as wanting to willingly live under communism.

Unfortunately, as I had swiftly discovered on more than a few occasions, being a conservative dater meant that I wasn't 'woke' enough to be loved. I had deleted Grindr from my phone and the very consciousness of my mind – never to be downloaded or spoken of again. But in-between Uber and Candy Crush, there was still Tinder temptingly lurking on my phone, an app which I had not used since my encounter with the exasperating spice boy.

Being treated like a political apparition and being erased from existence had left me licking my wounds, especially after the detrimental date that I had just been on with Harry, who had left our date in a fluster of natural gas and hot air – simply because I called him out on his green deal hypocrisy. But not wanting to be a victim and feel sorry for myself, I simply dusted myself, kept calm, and got on with it – even committing myself to another date in the process. It was a Friday afternoon in Liverpool Street station, and I found myself surrounded by bleary-eyed office workers in pinstriped suits leisurely slurping on their caffeine fix amid a rare sighting of sun, whilst unmindful tourists hopelessly attempted to top up their Oyster card as a queue of impatient Brits quietly huffed in syndication behind them.

Feeling choked by the obscene amount of people circling me and wishing that I had stayed in bed, I had agreed to go on a date with Lorenzo, a twenty-nine-year-old Personal Assistant and Italian national residing in Hackney. This was quite an impulsive date as we had only literally matched on Tinder the night before without as much of an exchange of political philosophy or our views on Margaret Thatcher's domestic policies of privatisation, so I was going into foreign territory in not knowing my date's political alliance.

I waited just outside of Liverpool Street station beneath the towering skyscrapers for my date to arrive, as I found myself once again stupidly early and waiting around for someone who could potentially turn out to be a fruitcake. I proceeded to do the monotonous routine of checking my WhatsApp to see if I had received a message from my late date, only for my phone to unexpectedly begin ringing with an anonymous number. "Hey… it's me," gushed a foreign-sounding accent as I tried to grasp who the voice belonged to. "I'm here, where are you?" asked the persistent voice on the phone, as I finally put two and two together and registered that it was Lorenzo.

"I'm by the entrance of the station, next to the escalators," I replied, as I scouted around to see if I could see someone who vaguely resembled what I remembered Lorenzo to look like from his Tinder photos. "Cool," Lorenzo swiftly replied. "I'll be there in a few minutes," he concluded, as I waited for my inventible date to arrive. So far so good, I thought to myself, as I attempted to appear as conspicuous as possible while waiting for my date to find me.

Lorenzo didn't sound like a lisping queer and fortunately sounded masculine with his virile Italian accent. But apart from a few photos and a vague bio on his Tinder profile that mentioned his love for travelling, I didn't know anything about my date, apart from the fact that he was born and raised in the city of Milan. So, with that in mind, I was expecting a gallant Italian man to sweep me off my feet and carry me off into the sunset as I looked around to see if Lorenzo was close by. But, as a small figure in the distance walked towards my direction, those fantasies of a strapping Italian man soon became just another unrealistic delusion relegated between Sadiq Khan and the tooth fairy.

"Hey there, how are you?" said a voice with the same sturdy accent that I spoke to on the phone a few minutes ago, as I was greeted with a hug from the minuscule man now mere metres away from me. But while receiving a hug was a nice way to start a spontaneous date, the fact that my date's arms barely reached the height of my nipples made me wish I hadn't been so impetuous and agreed to go on a date with someone who was seemingly the size of a garden gnome.

Measuring in at a microscopic 5 ft 2, Lorenzo was an absolute midget, and while height was never really a deal-breaker when it came to dating, being in a relationship with someone only a few feet higher than Danny DeVito was never really on the top of my list for qualities I looked for in a boyfriend.

The prospect of spending an afternoon with a pint-sized troll was not something that filled my stomach with romance and butterflies, especially when his profile clearly stated that he was at least 5 ft 8. But being the etiquette Englishman that I was, I replied to my diminutive date in a way that showed no signs of disappointment and despair and the fact that I had been well and truly catfished by an apparent hobgoblin.

"Great to meet you," I smiled while showing no signs of suicidal tendencies as we made our way to the destination of any true intimate first date... Nando's.

The last time I had been on a date to a Nando's restaurant, I was eating peri chicken with a non-binary person who had miraculously transformed into a transsexual woman overnight. And as luck would have it, I was now on a date with an elf who had to hoist his neck up just to make eye contact with me. As we began to make small talk (literally) on the way to the restaurant, it suddenly dawned on me that if by the doubtful probability that cupid's arrow somehow managed to strike us both as we tucked into our butterfly burgers and grilled halloumi cheese, I would have to inexplicable submerge my neck as low as possible to even attempt to have a conversation with him if we stood next to one another.

The unfortunate height difference was a shame, as despite having the build and height of an infant, Lorenzo was a good-looking guy, with piercing green eyes and a neatly trimmed beard with black quaffed hair and small framed glasses perched on his nose. And even though he was lacking in the size department, Lorenzo certainly had a particularly good sense of style, even if his clothes were likely from the boy's section in Primark. As we arrived at the restaurant and ordered our food, I learned a lot about my small-scale companion sitting across from me.

Lorenzo had moved to the UK from the sun-kissed surroundings of his home country and inadvertently found himself amongst the socialist brotherhood in the People's Republic of Hackney. Coming to the city of London to seek his fortune like many EU nationals who dreamt of a life in the vibrant and multicultural city, Lorenzo instead found a city plagued with knife crime, chavs, and far too many chicken shops, as he struggled to pay his rent on time for the 'privilege' of living in the bustling capital while sharing a tensely compact bathroom with Eastern European migrants in the middle of a crime-ridden multicultural ghetto.

After we both had polished off our plates in mostly awkward silence, I diverged on to the subject that was prohibited from being discussed on any first date – exes. But as this was a date that was never going to develop into anything more than a case study as to why pre-date social media background checks should be mandatory, I was willing to tread onto the hallowed forbidden grounds of talking about past relationships with someone whom I had no romantic interest in what so ever. And surprisingly, despite the height, or lack thereof, Lorenzo had quite the extensive list of past lovers and boyfriends, in which he boastfully began to list in numerical order and the length of time together in which they lasted, as I listened on in silence.

"I was with my last boyfriend Marcus for six months, but he accused me of cheating on him," dramatically revealed Lorenzo, as my date rattled on about his love life as if he was on an episode of Jerry Springer. "All I ever did was put my arm around his best friend after he drunkenly made a pass at me," swore an abashed Lorenzo, as he shrugged his shoulders in indifference over being caught in a compromising position with his boyfriend's best friend.

Throughout the date, Lorenzo managed to go through the entire cycle of his exes and previous relationships, and all before my cheesecake had arrived at the table. As I hesitantly listened to Lorenzo waffle on about his past conquests as if he was some kind of stud, I began to understand why they all ended up dumping him.

It wasn't because he was falsely accused of inappropriately touching the drunk best friend of a boyfriend who made a pass at him, or even because of his height, but evidently, it was because he had an exaggerated sense of his importance and was a clear example of short man syndrome – a complex found in short men who often ended up being overly-aggressive compulsive liars due to their physical shortcomings.

Lorenzo was the archetype of short man syndrome as he listed the 'achievements' of all his previous relationships as if he was some kind of irresistible Italian lothario.

Wanting to test the short man syndrome theory out, I moved the conversation onto a subject that I knew would provoke a fiery reaction from a midget European national with an attitude... Brexit. "So, what are your thoughts on Brexit?" I asked Lorenzo, knowing full well the consequences of asking such an explosive question could have catastrophic repercussions.

"Well, I think that the whole Brexit thing is pretty much rooted in xenophobia, to tell you the truth," Lorenzo admitted, seemingly unaware that he was currently on a date in the middle of Nando's with a Brexiteer and an apparent 'xenophobe'.

"Well, considering that I voted to leave in the referendum and am currently on a date with a conceited Italian midget, I guess that would make me a total xenophobe too, right?" I abruptly snapped, as all previous English etiquette and courteousness were instantaneously thrown out the window – along with any consideration I had of not wanting to offend someone with my political views who was willing to casually label 17.4 million people who voted in a national referendum as xenophobic.

Call it the frustration of being on a date with someone so self-absorbed and narcissistic, or the annoyance of being lambasted once again as some kind of hateful bigot for voting in a democratic referendum, but by this point, I had simply had enough of being patronised by a condescending dwarf over my political views. "I beg your pardon!" gasped Lorenzo, now staring at me from across the table with his mouth wide open in shock. "You heard me!" I angrily rebuked, now looking directly into his eyes as steam smeared the lenses of his glasses. "How can you sit there and call people xenophobic for wanting independence and the ability to govern their own country?" I angrily questioned, as I swiftly took a sip from my glass of Pepsi while still staring intensely at Lorenzo, who by now looked so startled it was as if he had unintentionally just seen Nicola Sturgeon's ginger minge.

I had been labelled a Nazi by Ronald for being a fan of his democratically elected President and smeared by a spice boy who probably didn't even know the difference between socialism and a 'Zigazig ah', but after the umpteenth time of sitting across from a date who found fault with my political views, I had visibly had enough and erupted in a frenzied fury that took my timid date by surprise.

There was an awkward silence in the air as Lorenzo took a sip from his drink while doing his utmost best not to make eye contact with me, as I took a deep breath while stubbornly doing my best not to make eye contact with him too. We both sat there what felt like an eternity as we both looked in all manner of directions except our own – avoiding even the slightest of eye contact as if we were both trying to avoid chlamydia.

It had been approximately fourteen minutes since I had scorned my date for insinuating that I had some kind of prejudice against people from other countries until we finally locked eyes and resumed communication.

"Honestly, I can't believe that I am on a date with someone who voted for Brexit," muttered Lorenzo, as he looked at me with the kind of repugnance one would have if they saw an unflushed toilet with over flowering diarrhoea spilling out.

"Well, I can't believe that I am on a date with someone so small that you could easily fit into my pocket," I replied bluntly, as I arched my eyebrow and continued to stare at Lorenzo from across the table. If this was an intense game of chess, then we were both at a stalemate with neither of us prepared to budge. Lorenzo seemingly despised me because I had used my democratic vote in a national referendum in which he was displeased over the outcome, while I, in turn, disliked the fact that he had blatantly lied about his height on Tinder and had accused me of being xenophobic when that couldn't have been further from the truth. As the waitress came to our table to collect our plates, I used the distraction to put my phone in my coat pocket before proceeding to get up from my chair.

"Oh, so you are going now?" gasped Lorenzo, as he looked up at me with a look of shock while still sitting firmly in his chair. "Well, I'm not going to stay on a date that is the equivalent of watching paint dry," I replied snidely, as I made my way to the entrance of the restaurant. But before I could make my way through the threshold of the entrance, I suddenly felt a slight tug on my coat only to procced to turn around to see Lorenzo standing there.

"Do you want to go for a drink?" he coyly suggested, while looking up at me like some kind of lost little puppy found in a ditch by the RSPCA. I was shocked, I had just been accused of being filled with unwavering hatred and disdain for foreigners because I was a Brexiteer, yet that very same foreigner who made that untrue claim was now asking me out for a drink. I don't know what it was that made me feel sorry for my dinky date as he pleaded with me to have a drink with him. Maybe it was the dejection in his green eyes that made my heart melt like low-fat butter as I pondered over how harshly I had treated him over our political differences.

Back to back dates in which I had been ridiculed over my political leanings had seemingly transformed me into a hard-hearted unmerciful brute and far removed from who I was when I originally decided to download Tinder. It's funny how countless bad dates and being called a racist and a Nazi could turn a cynic into even the most optimistic of people. And yet here I was, with one foot out of the door and ready to exit as Lorenzo stood with bated breath and looking like he was about ready to cry as he anxiously waited for my response. "Sure," I replied, as I moved my foot back through the threshold of the restaurant door. "I suppose one drink won't hurt," I smiled, as Lorenzo hurriedly made his way back to the table to collect his coat before we made our way out of the restaurant together.

We eventually found ourselves in The Admiral's Arms, a small traditional English pub just ten minutes away from Liverpool Street Station. Finding an empty table in the corner, we shuffled past a group of young men amid conversation as we sat down at our chairs and gave one another a reassuring smile. One hour and three gin and tonics later and I had officially elapsed into a state of absolute drunkenness, as a barely sober Lorenzo looked on in amusement at the sight of a stereotypical English drunk living up to every cliché intoxicated British tourist acting like a drunken prat in Ibiza.

"You know, I'm not normally like this," I drunkenly mumbled, as I took another sip of my drink while being barely able to string a coherent sentence together. They say that blurred vision while being under the influence of alcohol can turn even the most repulsive person into a stunner, and an hour into being absolutely sloshed and Lorenzo had miraculously grown a whole ten feet in height. Hallucinating a gigantic Italian stallion soaring over me, I abruptly lunged at Lorenzo while uncompromisingly sticking my tongue down his throat in the process.

Quite possibly in shock but not opposed to the prospect of snogging a boozed-up Brexiteer who was supposedly xenophobic over an hour ago, Lorenzo reciprocated my drunken wooing technique and we ended up making out in the corner of the pub. After five-minutes of tonsil tennis and desperately needing air, I pulled back from the grip of Lorenzo's mouth and quickly sobered up, realising that I had been inappropriately engaging in public displays of affection with a dwarf. But rather than holding my head in shame over my lack of conservative public conduct, I simply shrugged my shoulders and re-entered my tongue into Lorenzo's little mouth.

A strange feeling took over my body as I found myself eclipsing the disapproving glare of Margaret Thatcher immersed in the depths of my mind – continuing to exchange drool with a diminutive Italian in public. I felt unrestricted as I dreamingly closed my eyes and envisioned that I was in some type of romantic Italian novel, as the sound of our lips kissing collided like waves on the ocean shore.

After imagining that I was walking barefoot through the Amalfi Coast with an Italian hunk, I was suddenly snapped out of my drunken delirium by the sound of laughing, as I took another gasp of breath and pulled away from Lorenzo and turned around to see that we were being watched by a gawking group of businessmen who found the sight of two men rowdily kissing in the corner of the pub amusing.

"Why don't we go somewhere else?" whispered Lorenzo in my ear, as I awkwardly tried not to look up at the group of men staring at us as if we were a homoerotic installation in the Tate Modern. "But where?" I asked Lorenzo, as I perched myself back into my seat while attempting to regain some decorum. "Come with me," smiled Lorenzo, as he beckoned me to follow him.

CHAPTER 12

DEMOCRACY IN THE DARK

I could hear the faint sound of muffled music blaring from inside of the derelict building that we were standing outside of as I looked around with squinted eyes trying to suss out where the hell I was. We had arrived in Brick Lane, an area once associated with the downtrodden slums and the infamous blood-soaked scene in which Jack the Ripper brutally murdered slum-dwelling prostitutes before abdominally mutilating his unwilling victims.

Not wanting to particularly have my throat cut and my body organs harvested and sold on the Russian black market, I cautiously asked Lorenzo what were we doing here – looking around at what could only be best described as absolute squalor. "This is a club," revealed Lorenzo, as he finally disclosed what was within the crumbling concealed building that we found ourselves idly standing outside of. As I looked at the neglected planks of rotted wood holding the deteriorating and fragile timber roof that housed the entrance to this monstrously of a building, I questioned as to why a club would be situated in such a rundown part of the city. "A club?" I gasped in shock, as the sound of creaking wood began to grate when an abrupt gush of wind blew through the air. "A special kind of club actually," smiled Lorenzo, as a devilish grin proceeded to materialize across his face.

Arousing my curiosity of what exactly a 'special club' was, I further questioned Lorenzo as to what exactly was lurking behind the dilapidated construction towering before me. "Come inside and find out," urged Lorenzo, as he proceeded to take me by the hand and lead me towards the stained steel entrance doors of the building.

Lorenzo knocked on the door with a heavy three taps on the blue shaded steel door, as he turned around while looking at me with the same devilish grin that he flashed across his face a few moments ago. We waited for what seemed like only a few moments before an anonymous voice muttered from the other side of the locked door. "Password?" asked the faceless voice, as I stood stiffly behind Lorenzo while anxiously wondering if I was about to enter the secret headquarters of some kind of cannibalistic satanic cult or worst yet, the Green Party headquarters.

"Down boy," responded Lorenzo, as the sound of a bolt being unlocked echoed from behind the steel door before slowly creaking open and revealing a blackened passageway where the shadowy figure of a person beneath a flickering light stood. "Welcome to Escapade," smiled Lorenzo, as I gazed down the dark winding corridor, which could only be best described as staring down the pathway to the kingdom of Hades. Lorenzo took my hand and proceeded to walk through the threshold of the door as I apprehensively walked behind him while tightly gripping his hand as if my life depended on it. As we got through the door and made our way through the damp passageway, the shadowy outline of the person under the flickering light became more transparent, and while I was half expecting a hulking bouncer with an intimidating glare and a rugged beard, what I was not expecting was a hulking bouncer with an intimidating glare and a rugged beard wearing a dress. "Hey Lorenzo, good to see you again," gushed the anonymous figure, as the flickering light reflected off the bright pink bodycon dress that the pot-bellied man had squeezed into, with strands of chest hair straying from out of the exhaustedly squeezed tight-fitting frock wrapped around his burly body.

We made our way past the bearded man in the dress and continued to walk down the darkened narrow corridor as I stumbled through the blackness while half-expecting to abruptly fall flat on my face.

There were no lights leading the way along the corridor other than the one flickering lightbulb that steadily swung above the unidentified bearded lady who we had long walked past. I began to feel feverishly claustrophobic as we both continued walking through the confined corridor that felt like it was getting narrower and narrower as we proceeded onwards.

After what seemed like an eternity of walking through absolute nothingness, there was suddenly a glimmer of light at the end of the tunnel as we walked towards what looked like a metallic door basked under a blue dimmed light – the dwindled sound of music coming from behind the door growing louder with each passing step.

"Well, here we are," announced Lorenzo, as we promptly stopped at the foot of the door. "And where is here?" I curiously replied, as I looked at Lorenzo, who was now subdued in the shade of the blue light hanging above the door. "You'll soon see," he smirked, as he put his hand onto the metallic door and proceeded to push it open. I could feel the vibrations of the music playing from behind the door quiver throughout my body while a feeble creaking sound softy filled the narrow corridor as the door slowly opened.

Lorenzo continued to push the door wide open until it was fully unlatched, when, all of a sudden, a whiff of cigarette smoke raced towards me as the sound of pulsing music erupted in my eardrums.

I looked through the opened door in astonishment as if I had just opened the wardrobe from the tales of The Lion, the Witch, and the Wardrobe. But instead of intensely gazing upon the enchanted surroundings of snowy sprinkled trees and ice-capped mountains found within the other-worldly closet in the fables of the Chronicles of Narnia, I instead found myself fixedly gazing upon the outrageous events that were happening before my very own eyes.

There was a large room with the walls painted in a shadowy red as a mass of scantily clad and naked men engaged in perverse positions and what could only be bluntly described as rabid sexual penetration, while the sound of deafening techno music played over the dry-ice smoke swirled in an array of blue and acid green laser lights shooting above the scene of bare fused bodies tangled in the act of expeditious sex. And then the penny finally dropped – Lorenzo had brought me to a gay sex club.

There were naked men frantically kissing other naked men while gyrating their bodies against one another as I looked on in astonishment. Men in nothing but suspenders and heels thrust themselves onto vigorous muscled men with biceped arms and an entranced peer as they sat bare and legs apart whilst their hands leisurely groped the raw-boned body that was seductively frolicking on top of them. In the corner, and unashamedly in full view of every one was four rugged and unclothed men breathlessly engaged in frenziedly penetrative sex with one another as the sounds of whimpering and exhilarated moans blended in with the pulsating beats of the music. I was standing dumbfounded by the entrance of a room in which everyone was undressed or completely nude and performing unimaginable sexual acts on one another without guilt. But before I could catch my bearings and evaluate what I was going to do next, I suddenly felt a light tap on my shoulder from a touch of a hand, only to swiftly turn around and proceed to go into an immediate state of shock, as the sight of Lorenzo stripped and completely stark naked fixedly stared back up at me.

"Why don't you join me?" sniggered Lorenzo, as I awkwardly tried to keep my eyesight firmly locked into his eyes and not stare at his penis. "No, I'm fine, thank you," I nervously giggled, as I tried desperately to still not look down at Lorenzo's bare-naked manhood which was ferociously pointing at me and was now semi-erect. "Oh, that's a shame," responded Lorenzo, before briskly turning around and heading off towards a blue coloured door on the other end of the room – catching a full-frontal glimpse of his bare buttocks in the process.

I remained paused as I scanned the room whilst still paralysed with disbelief over where I was and what was occurring around me. The muddled sounds of throbbing beats and sexualised moans blurred my mind as I frantically tried to figure out what to do next. Lorenzo had seemingly abandoned me and ventured through a mysterious blue door at the opposite end of the room which lead to who knows where, as I uncomfortably stood next to a slender gentleman performing oral sex to another man who was wearing nothing but red coloured thigh high latex boots and an engraved look of ecstasy on his face. I was just about to make my way back through the entrance in which I had arrived when I felt another faint touch of a hand on my shoulder. "Excuse me," said a mild-mannered voice, as I promptly turned around to see a fully dressed man smiling back at me. "You look lost," laughed the man, who was dressed in a smart pair of trousers with brown leather shoes and a grey woollen jumper – not the kind of attire that one would expect somebody to wear in an unrestrained gay sex club. "I am lost," I laughed back, as I proceeded to shrug my shoulders in dubiety. "I know the feeling," admitted the smartly dressed man, as the smell of pungent sweat and body odour lingered throughout the room as if we were in some kind of sweltering sauna. "So, what is someone so well dressed doing in a gay sex club?" I teased, as I leaned in closer to avoid being drowned out by the monotonous techno music blaring over the speakers of the club. "I came here unintentionally with a mate, but it seems that I have lost him," chuckled the well turned out man, as I looked on with a knowing sympathetic smile.

The spruced and rather dapper-looking man was Nick, a twenty-seven-year-old investment banker working in Canary Wharf, the bustling business district of London, and not the kind of suited professional you would imagine to willingly venture into a sex club on a Friday afternoon, well, not unless your name was Prince Andrew anyway.

After a few back and fourths in what was a considerably conventional conversation surrounded by titillated and impassioned homosexual men, I learnt that Nick was not a regular to Escapade but instead was heedlessly dragged along by a work colleague who had heard through the grapevine that there was an illegal gay sex club in the dodgy end of Brick Lane.

Nick brought us two pints of Guinness at the bar, and before you know it, we were having a civilised dialogue with one another next to an exposed paunchy middle-aged man casually masturbating by himself as we discussed everything from Thatcherism, Brexit, and even the 1997 United Kingdom general election in which Tony Blair took his first steps in realising his dastardly plan of a globalist Britain. Amongst aroused homosexual men placing their genitalia in places on the body I never knew existed, I had inadvertently found somebody who was politically neutral and tolerant of differing social views. Nick was what you would call objective when it came to the current political landscape, which in recent years had become nothing more than a tribal battleground of warring political parties and political commentators trying to outdo one another in a desperate battle for tweets and attention. Nick didn't burst into flames when I mentioned my love for President Trump, nor did he run a mile when I told him that I had voted to leave the European Union either.

"I voted to remain, but I respect the result of the referendum," revealed Nick, as the roaring sound of someone climaxing to an orgasm erupted a few seats away.

Nick was unprejudiced, non-partisan, and was able to hold an intellectual conversation without coming down with a severe case of Trump derangement syndrome. And if that wasn't good enough, he was also very good-looking.

Nick's dark brown eyes sparkled with laughter as I recalled the disastrous bad date that I had just been on with Lorenzo, who curiously had still not reappeared from behind the concealed blue door since he left me.

"I bet your date is having a real good time behind that door," giggled Nick, as he firmly gripped his glass and took a sip of his drink. "So, what exactly is behind that door?" I questioned Nick, as I looked over from where we were sitting and gazed at the anonymous blue door that was on the other end of the room. "It's a dark room," proclaimed Nick, as I looked at him with a puzzled expression on my face. "What is a dark room?" I asked as I racked my brain as to what exactly a dark room could be. "You really are a Tory, aren't you?" laughed Nick, as he placed his glass of Guinness firmly on the table.

Nick explained that a darkroom was a pitch-black room bathed in complete darkness in which occupants could have sex with someone under the guise of complete anonymity without even knowing who they were or what they looked like. The thought of poking my bits inside unidentified people left a lot to be desired, as I recoiled at the prospect of what Lorenzo was probably getting up to behind that concealed blue door.

Imagine thinking you were getting a blowjob from a spunky contestant from Love Island only to register that Diane Abbott had been slurping on your penis the entire time, as I shuddered at the prospect of ejaculating in the mouth of someone who couldn't even coordinate their shoes correctly. While the concept of the darkroom was enough to give anyone nightmares, I was strangely intrigued as to know how it felt like to be immersed in complete blackness.

I had always imagined what it must feel like to be completely incognito and not to be judged or scrutinised for my political leanings under the anonymity of absolute darkness, that I felt myself becoming more fascinated as to what could be lurking behind that concealed blue door.

"Hey, why don't we go inside?" I wildly suggested to Nick, as the prospect of being completely inconspicuous in utter darkness left me feeling too curious to resist.

"Are you sure?" questioned Nick, who was probably more shocked over the fact that a Tory would dare want to do something so outrageous as to explore a dark room in a gay sex club. "Yes, I'm very sure," I laughed, as I proceeded to get up from off the seats that we were sat on while eagerly pulling Nick up by the arm with me. I swiftly led Nick as I navigated our way through the crowd of perspiring naked men that had congregated on the dancefloor and headed towards the entrance of the darkroom. I almost slipped on what could have been either semen or a spilt drink on the dancefloor as I traversed through the last remaining huddled bodies of naked men fiddling with themselves under the strobe lights as we made our way outside the blue concealed of the darkroom.

"Well, I'm a gentleman, so you can go in first," smiled Nick, as I let go of his wrist and gazed upon the infamous blue door that held from behind its closed entryway a shadowy netherworld from within. I suddenly found myself feeling nervous as I gazed upon the intimidating door of the darkroom where just a few moments ago I had been full of exuberance in exploring the great unknown.

Not wanting to embarrass myself in front of Nick, who I had just dragged over to arouse my curiosity, I took a deep breath and placed my hand onto the handle of the door – my hand feeling slightly unsteady as I proceeded to pull the door open. "Go on, you can do it," laughed Nick, as I steadily pulled the door wide open and found myself suddenly staring into complete darkness.

I felt a grip on my hand as I looked down to see that Nick had firmly gripped my sweaty palm, as I looked back into the ominous darkness. "I'll look after you," smiled Nick, as he looked at me reassuringly. I replied with a faint smile but a smile not reassuring enough to garner any confidence in what I was about to do, as I put my right foot into the smouldering blackness before immersing myself into the darkness.

With Nick still firmly grasping on to my hand, we both fully walked into the room and across the threshold as the door behind us slowly began to close. The last remaining strands of light from the dancefloor began to deteriorate before the door firmly closed all the way shut before we suddenly found ourselves completely absorbed in complete and utter blackness. "Are you OK?" asked Nick, as I gripped his hand as eagerly as Joe Biden grabbing the hand of a prepubescent girl. "I'm OK," I whispered while imagining that this is what it must look like to be inside the mind of a Green Party voter – absolute emptiness.

We walked further and further into the darkness as our footsteps echoed along what seemed like a long and winding corridor. "Where does this lead to?" I quietly whispered to Nick – not wanting to draw any attention from whoever was engulfed in the dense blackness with us. "I have no idea," replied Nick quietly, as he firmly held tight of my jittery hand to assure me that he was still beside me. I was walking with my other arm firmly stretched out in front of me as my hand grasped unfamiliarly into the rampant darkness – not knowing what I may touch or stumble across in the lingering darkness. However, it only took a few more steps before we came across our first sign of life amongst the shadows, as the faint sound of murmuring echoed from the distance.

We walked further and further into the darkness, when suddenly, and without warning, we were hit by the sounds of heavy breathing and moaning occurring from all around us. We had seemingly reached our destination as we stood still in complete silence occupied in the darkness – listening carefully to the sound of heavy petting and skin being smacked that was transpiring around us.

Some of the noises that could be heard from the limbo of blackness resembled animalistic mating sounds as men savagely penetrated anonymous men under the guise of complete darkness. One of those men being ferociously manhandled was Lorenzo, who among the bodies of men plunged in darkness was probably engrossed in the throes of intimacy, as I stood there under the veil of darkness in complete shock and disbelief.

I almost felt sorry for Lorenzo and those who had to come to a room gripped in absolute darkness just so they could feel some kind of sexual arousal with an unidentified participant, especially if it turned out that the person who had ejaculated all over their face looked like Shrek. I had satisfied my curiosity and was ready to leave when Nick abruptly began to laugh. "Margaret Thatcher would be spinning in her grave if she saw a Tory in a dark room in a gay sex club," chuckled Nick, as I cackled at the prospect of the Iron Lady disapproving of how far I had ventured off the Tory path and into utter madness. But as soon as Nick had spoken the words 'Tory' out of his mouth, the surrounding sounds of rampant exhaling and hefty breathing immediately stopped.

You could hear a needle drop as we stood there in total silence surrounded by darkness when suddenly, an anonymous voice bellowed "Tory!?" from the shadows. We both paused in shock, as I tightly gripped Nick's hand. "What the fuck is a Tory doing here?!" screamed the same anonymous voice, as I stood immobilized in fear.

Neither myself nor Nick uttered a word as the same screeching voice angrily yelled, "If there is a Tory in here, I am going to fuck you up!" as my heart began to promptly race. There I was, standing benumbed in the middle of a dark room with naked homosexual men engaging in rampant sex with one another around me under the shroud of darkness, and I had just been physically threatened by an unidentified person simply because I was a Tory.

I had been ridiculed, criticised, mocked, and dumped over my political views, but to be intimidated with the possibility of physical assault in a dark room by someone who just a few moments ago had probably been fondling unknowingly with the genitals of a morbidly obese pensioner was a new low for me.

But before I had time to quietly tiptoe my way out of there without being suspected, I suddenly felt an instant splash of liquid hurled in my face. "Got him!" roared the faceless voice amidst the darkness, as the cold liquid that had been hurled in my face dripped down from my eyes down to my chin. Gobsmacked over what had just happened, I rapidly let go of Nick's hand and immediately touched my face with both hands while hastily wiping the dripping liquid away from my eyes. The liquid that had been deliberately tossed into my face had seemingly been an alcohol beverage, as the whiff of what smelt like beer settled on my face. I had just been physically assaulted by someone who had developed the ability to spot a Tory in the dark, as the last drips of alcohol trickled from my chin and onto my t-shirt. "Fucking Tory scum!" scolded the anonymous voice from the darkness, as I cowered in fear and promptly covered my face for fear of having any other unidentified liquids hurled in my face by an apparent anti-Tory thug who could seemingly smell the whiff of Thatcherism amongst the stench of semen and sweat.

I hurriedly turned around, putting both of my arms up with widened palms stretched out in front of me and swiftly retraced my previous steps in a hastily attempt to get out of there.

"George, where are you?" Nick yelled from the darkness, as I speedily walked through the blackened corridor and towards the entrance of the darkroom. In that moment of panic and trepidation, I didn't care about Nick – abruptly leaving him alone in the spot in which I had just been aggressively drenched for being a Tory.

I just wanted to escape the darkness and break free from the perverted grip of Escapade, as I hurried nervously through the bleak of darkness, desperately trying to find the way out of the darkroom.

"Where is that fucking Tory scum!?" angrily yelled the same faceless voice, as I frighteningly sped up my footsteps in an attempt to flee from the anonymous thug who seemingly wanted to have my guts for garters – walking faster and faster through the shadows. I continued to hold my hands out in desperation when suddenly I felt the touch of what felt like a door. I scrambled anxiously looking for a handle in complete darkness before finally grasping the handle of the door and hurriedly pushing it open.

My vision was blurry as I stepped across the threshold and out of the darkness while my eyesight adjusted back to my surroundings – finding myself back in the main room of the club as strobe lights flickered off the bodies of naked men still intertwined in the firm grip of fornication. With excessive speed, I pushed myself past the horde of sweaty bodies and hastily made my way up to the exit of the club – still traumatised over what had just occurred in the darkroom as I madly pushed the entrance door open and finding myself back in the same blue-lit narrow corridor that I had previously trudged along with Lorenzo by my side.

The thumping sounds of my running footsteps echoed the damped corridor as I sprinted past the bulky man in the pink dress who had previously granted myself and Lorenzo access to Escapade – extending out my arm and reaching out my sweaty hand before bolting the stained steel entrance door wide open and racing out into the outside.

I stopped for a moment to catch my breath as the intense tightening feeling in my chest began to ease. It was still daylight as I looked around at the scatted garbage from ravaged bin bags that had been littered across the pavement of this neglected part of Brick Lane that I once again found myself in as I took out my phone and glanced at my screen to see what time it was.

I had been inside the darkened clutches of Escapade for almost two hours and, in my frightened haste to avoid further political escalation from occurring in the darkroom, I had forgotten to get Nick's number. I had two important life-altering choices that I could make as I gazed upon the menacing concealed building that I had just narrowly scarpered from.

I could brave the horror that lied within – despite the obscene amount of sexually transmitted disease that festered from within this towering and intimidating structure, and not to mention the frightening possibility of coming face to face with my anonymous attacker who might be able to recognise me by the fear and alcohol dripping from my face. Or I could wait outside the impoverished barren streets of Brick Lane until the early hours of the morning when Nick would finally emerge from the darkened shadows and awkwardly attempt to get his phone number, even if I did just hurriedly scurry away and leave him in a darkroom with not as much as a goodbye. In the end, I decided to hot-foot it out of Brick Lane where I found myself miles away from the shadows of the darkness and immersed under the bright lights of the swaying carriage.

CHAPTER 13

LABOUR PAINS

I was always under the impression that Labour MP's were holier-than-thou and immersed in such virtuous superiority and wokeness that they wouldn't even hurt a fly, let alone misgender a poor victimised insect and hurt its feelings. So, you can imagine my shock when I received an unsolicited picture of an erected penis in my inbox from a Labour Member of Parliament who I had just inadvertently matched with on Tinder.

Bryan Lewis, Labour MP of a London Borough tucked in-between the poverty of Haringey and the superiority of Islington had just sent me an unprompted photo of the most unfortunately sized penis that I had ever seen. However, it wasn't just the abnormal genitalia that was the most perplexing thing about this whole situation, but the fact that he had even matched and messaged me at all, which was the most peculiar thing about this awkward situation that I had inadvertently found myself in.

What was even more awkward (apart from the slightly off coloured tiny penis) was the fact that we had both already met before. I first met Bryan when I canvassed for the Conservative Party in a neighbouring borough a few years back.

Bryan was a local Labour councillor and had canvassed in opposition of the Conservative Party, often resulting in underhanded tactics in ensuring that our leaflets would not be distributed around the area.

One time, he had even instructed a Labour Party volunteer to steal a box of our promotional material and disregard it in the bins behind the local kebab house, as the Labour Party continued its stranglehold in the borough by using dirty and underhanded tactics.

Unfortunately for local Conservative Party residents, Bryan would eventually go on to become MP for the area by quite a substantial margin – which just goes to show that there was no accounting for taste when it came to the local people of North London. So, despite Bryan deliberately sabotaging our election campaign, it was rather weird to be looking at a picture of his microscopic penis staring back at me – especially when he had been such an utter dick to me the last time that I saw him.

My stained t-shirt, which I had worn when I had alcohol abruptly hurled in my face in the darkroom had been swirling around the washing machine and was ridden of any unscrupulous stains of that aforementioned night.

Lorenzo, who had originally brought me to Escapade and who had mysteriously disappeared into the blackness of the darkroom and never to be seen or heard from again, had blocked me from WhatsApp. So, going on a date with a perverted Labour MP with a minuscule penis seemed only fitting, considering that I had just been on a date with an Italian dwarf in a gay sex club.

However, by the sounds of his rambling and sexually explicit messages, it seemed that the local Labour MP wasn't looking for enduring love and romance, but instead was looking to fulfil his unusual perverted desire to have sex with a Brexiteer.

"My fantasy is to get so fucking railed up with a Brexiteer that we end up having the most mind-blowing and extraordinary sex ever while I fuck my frustration out on him for voting us out of the EU," described Bryan in detail, as he relayed his sick intention to penetrate the politics out of my brain.

While the prospect of engaging in some kind of sadistic role play under the bedsheets with my political adversary did intrigue me, I ended up swiftly deleting Bryan's number from my phone.

To be honest, I had seen enough warped and depraved sights just within the last week alone to last me a lifetime, so the prospect of a Labour MP aggressively suffocating me in the bedroom and getting turned on by it, while compelling, wasn't on the top of my list of priorities. It was a Saturday night, and I had been invited out by my Spanish flatmate Miguel to go to Camden for a few drinks.

Miguel was openly gay, and even though he was liberal and heavily active on the gay scene we got on pretty well and never clashed or came to blows when it came to our political differences.

He was a rare breed of cattle and was a proud member of the LGBT community who wasn't nutty as a rainbow fruitcake. We sat outside a bar that overlooked Camden Lock as the lights from the line of lightbulbs hanging across a set of trees flickered onto the peacefully still water of the canal.

"So, a Labour MP wants to have sex with me because I'm a Brexiteer," I laughed, as I recalled the proposition presented to me by the perverted politician. "What the fuck!" gasped Miguel, as he looked at me with complete bewilderment. "Yeah, apparently it's a sexual fantasy of his to have sex with someone who he politically despises," I continued, as I relayed to Miguel the suggested positions that Bryan wanted to perform with me while internally despising everything that I stood for.

There was a term for wanting to desperately rip off the clothes from someone that you passionately loathed, and that term was 'hate sex'.

Bryan hated my political views and the fact that I had voted to leave the European Union, so much so that he wanted to have sex with me to vent his democratic frustrations out on me for voting in a way that did not conform to his way of thinking. It was a sad state of the times that a Remainer and a Brexiteer having consensual sex together was now seen as a kink in a society that had lost all civil dialogue and tolerance for one another.

Not only had politics critically divided the nation and hindered romantic endeavours, but the likes of Brexit and Trump had also dampened out the flames in the bedroom department. Everyone was always so angry and full of enraged hate that they couldn't get their head around the fact that there was more to life than politics, and just because someone voted differently to you, it didn't make them a bad person.

Unfortunately, this was not the case, and if political adversaries weren't infuriatingly protesting outside Westminster against each other in the cold – they were consistently complaining over being offended over differing views that didn't quite align with their own. Maybe Bryan was on to something, maybe we all just needed to engage in a little bit of hate sex with our political rivals to help ease the rigidity and to help release the sexual tension that was internally brewing alongside the hatred for our democratic antagonists. "You never know, the sex could be hot," laughed Miguel, as he proceeded to give me the cheekiest of winks while inconspicuously advocating that I go and get penetrated by a pervy Labour MP.

However, he did have a point, while I had seen enough penises to last me a lifetime in the last week, there was something deliciously erotic about having sex with someone you would never share an election booth with. Bryan was not half bad looking for someone in their early forties, and, despite the receding hairline and problematic anti-Semitic views that were shared by most of his colleagues and beyond reprehensible, I found myself sexually drawn to him.

Miguel had firmly planted the seed into my mind that the sex between myself and Bryan could be mind-boggling, plus, I could firmly tick off the bucket list that I had sex with a Member of Parliament, even if they did just so happen to be a Labour MP. "I'm going to message him," I boldly announced to Miguel, as I scrambled to grab my phone from out of my coat pocket.

Once again, I had been possessed by the same rush of adrenaline and curiosity that had made me enter the depths of hell that was the darkroom in Escapade – as I scrolled back to find the last message in WhatsApp that Bryan had sent to me. While I had deleted his phone number, like any responsible and upstanding conservative would do, I still had his previous messages in which he went into not so subtle detail in how he would make me his 'submissive Tory slut'.

"Hey, it's George, how are you?" I briskly typed on WhatsApp, before nimbly sending off my uncomplicated message to the sexually freakish Labour MP – resaving his number on my phone book as I promptly wedged my phone back into my trouser pocket. "So, you're going to meet him?" asked Miguel curiously, as he looked at me with an intensely inspective gaze. "Let's see if he responds first," I replied smiling, as I looked out to the motionless stream of Camden Lock. While the flowing stream of the canal was in a state of quiescent, I was internally having a mild panic attack. I had just casually initiated the process of having sex with a Labour MP who wanted to sexually humiliate me because I had voted for Brexit. To say that this was a peculiar situation to find myself in was an understatement, as I took a firm gulp from my drink and gazed blankly into the distance.

I continued to drink obnoxiously priced cocktails alongside Camden Lock with Miguel as I noodled along with simulated intrigue upon learning that Kim Kardashian's selfie record was over one thousand in a single day by my Kardashian obsessed housemate. After two hours of listening non-stop to Kardashian propaganda, I decided to call it a night.

Miguel wanted to carry on drinking and had kindly invited me to go to Soho with him, where a few of his fellow Spanish friends were currently out partying. But feeling sleep deprived and not particularly excitable over the prospect of spending a night on the town with a group of inebriated homosexual Spaniards exaggeratedly gushing over Kylie Jenner's enormous lips, I said my goodbyes to Miguel as we went our separate ways at Camden Station.

I began to walk to the bus stop to catch the bus back to Hackney as I didn't fancy being uncomfortably squashed up beside an obese feminist on the Northern Line on a Saturday evening. I arrived at the bus stop with five minutes until my bus was due to arrive when I began to feel vibrations from the inside of my trouser pocket.

I expeditiously grabbed my phone from out of my trouser pocket while abruptly being overcome with anxiety as I began to second guess who could be calling me at this time of the evening. With my phone firmly in my hand, I flipped open the protective case to peek at the phone screen. And as I gazed upon the name of the caller flashing on my phone case, my anxiety abruptly hit the soaring heights of the stratosphere – Bryan was calling me! "Hello," I quietly answered, as sweat began to dispense from the palm of my quivering hand as I held the phone close to my ear.

"Hey, sexy Tory boy," the voice on the other end of the line teased back as I stood flustered by the bus timetable. Not only was a Labour MP calling me late in the evening, but he sounded somewhat concupiscent too as I replied. "Hey you dirty Labour MP," I giggled, as I embarked on what was seemingly political phone sex while situated near a bus stop in Camden. "So, are you free to meet now?" inquired an amorous Bryan, as I briskly looked at the phone screen to see what time it was. "But it's almost ten at night," I gasped while having already relished myself to the prospect of tea and toast on the sofa. "Oh, come on Tory boy, stop being such a boring conservative," insisted Bryan, as I recovered and licked my wounds from being perceived as a monotonous Tory.

Bryan had hit a slight nerve; while I was a proud Conservative Party voter, I was anything but boring. The fact that I had even crossed the threshold into the intimidating darkroom of Club Climax practically made me the self-certified Tory Bear Grylls, demonstrating my heroic and lionhearted courageousness by venturing deep into the pits of despair.

Even more impressive was that I was able to hold an articulate conversation with somebody in a gay sex club while a fat old man rapidly masturbated a few metres away and was surly a clear indicator of how much of a goody-goody I wasn't. Determined to prove to the perverted Labour MP that not all Tory's were toffy-nosed bores, I responded with all the perseverance of a Tory wanting to prove a point.

"So, how long will it take me to get to yours?" I asked Bryan, as the bus home to my night of tea and toast on the sofa abruptly drove right past me. Twenty minutes and two red signals later and I found myself in the ravaged wastelands of Tottenham. Walking through this part of London on a Saturday night is what I imagined Alice felt like when she first stumbled across that hallucinated talking rabbit and fell ass-first into the long and winding hole that resulted in her waking up in some kind of distorted and contorted version of a Labour Party conference.

The last time that I felt like a disorientated Alice was when I was being led astray by an Italian dwarf into the perverted darkness. But now I found myself amid veiled shadowy women who peed anonymously from behind their draping cloak, as I fearfully gazed around my surroundings which could only be best described as a nightmare. If this was diversity, then Tottenham was a strange mix of the unusual, the indigent and the terrifying.

It was also no surprise that this area had been a Labour stronghold and under the firm grip of MP David Lammy for what felt like centuries, and also probably the reason why it resembled the ruined remains of a post-apocalyptic dystopia. Tottenham was an area in London that any responsible adult would knowingly avoid like the plague, as I awkwardly found myself standing outside the entrance of Seven Sisters station waiting for Bryan to show up as hooded figures rode on bikes and circled the area like vultures searching for vulnerable prey

Tottenham was where the notorious London riots of 2011 had first originated from, in which masses of disgruntled youth burnt down buildings and looted local businesses while stealing everything from JD Sports trainers to basmati rice from Tesco while proudly showing off their stolen treasures on social media. Tottenham was also known for its growing violent crime, anti-social behaviour and mass-immigrant population, so the fact that I had unwillingly agreed to meet Bryan amongst the backdrop of betting shops and poverty demonstrated my commitment in showcasing that I was not a Tory bore – even if it was for the approval of a perverted Labour MP who treated my political views as some kind of corrupted kink. Tottenham certainly wasn't the multicultural utopia that the Labour Party had dreamingly ingrained on their socialist etch a sketch, but instead, accurately represented the decline of English culture and traditions in the outer suburbs of London, as the fantasy of immensely different cultures, religions and ethnicities living harmoniously together side by side without bitter disagreement and internalised unwavering hatred for one another became more and more transparent.

It was hard to ignore the differences amongst people with vastly contrasting values and cultures and the speed in which London was changing, as I found myself living in a city in which I was now the minority as a white Englishman. And while the left had tried their very best to forcibly blend these strikingly opposing qualities of life and call it multiculturalism, you certainly could see and feel the divergence when walking down a high-street in the outer suburbs of London – only to find yourself in a foreign land that felt far away from home.

Multiculturalism looked great in theory, but in the end, it did not work out so well in practice, often resulting in ghettoisation and segregation of different faiths and ethnicities who wanted to keep themselves isolated while creating gated communities in which outsiders were either shunned or expected to conform.

The influx of mass multiculturalism almost always resulted in sectarian tribes fighting to be the domineering force within their communities, often muscling their ideologies and cultures upon others with intimidation and fear.

Even German Chancellor Angela Merkel, who had opened the borders of Europe to a mass influx of immigrants from the Middle East and Africa during the migrant crisis of 2015, had admitted that her globalist attempt to create a multicultural society within her country of Germany had 'utterly failed' after those very same immigrants who pleaded for asylum refused to integrate into German culture. Instead, wanting to transform their generous hosts home into a duplicate of the country that they had reputedly fled from in fear and dismay. And while those who transcribed the doctrine of multiculturalism insisted that all cultures were of equal value and that no culture was superior or inferior to any other, when those very same cultures brought with them the act of female genital mutilation, child marriage, grooming gangs, honour killings or the tradition of 'Bacha Bazi', an act in which older men dressed younger and adolescent boys in dresses and sexually assaulted them, you had to question whether this was really culturally enriching or just western genocide.

And while there was no sign of young boys being forcibly dressed as fetishised women (or 'Drag Kids' as the left and LGBT community call it) there was a sinister-looking group of youths who were gawking at me from across the road as I tightly held my phone in the rigid grip of my quivering hand while waiting for Bryan to call me.

Not wanting to be another knife statistic in a city that had seen an unprecedented rise in crime, I speedily called Bryan from my phone. "Where are you?" I whispered, while desperately trying not to draw any more undesirable attention from the local hoodlum who looked like they were ready to pounce on me like ravaging animals.

Fortunately for me, just as I was about to be thuggishly ripped to shreds by the 'aspiring footballers' that had convened outside the station, Bryan walked around the corner, and at that moment, I couldn't have felt more relieved to have seen a Labour MP. "Hey, sorry I was late," pleaded Bryan, as he greeted me with the kind of puny embrace that most politicians would muster up when meeting constituents in a part of town that they didn't like. "It's fine," I sighed, while resorting to the same old tried and tested formula of the stiff upper lip, as I begrudgingly held onto my anger for being made to wait in a crime-stricken ghetto.

Under the flickering light of the faulty street lamppost, Bryan looked considerably skinnier than what I remembered him being the last time that I saw him. The stress of socialism had taken its toll on Bryan, as we engaged in idle chit-chat before I agreed to go back to his apartment.

Bryan's apartment was a ten-minute walk from the station, which meant that we had to trawl the darkened backstreets of Tottenham, as I intensely kept my eyes firmly in the back of my head. However, in a borough that had been voting for Labour since the dawn of time, I felt pretty safe in knowing that I was in the company of someone who was practically Jesus among the locals, as we made our way to his enshrined apartment. "So why don't you live in Camden?" I curiously asked Bryan, as we made our way through a grimy council estate. "Well, Tottenham is a lot cheaper to live in than Camden," Bryan laughed, as the sound of disused cans scattered across the wind-swept street.

Finally, after managing to walk through the mean streets of Tottenham without a single scratch or stab wound, we made it to Bryan's apartment, which astonishingly just so happened to be perched above an off-licence.

Even for a Labour MP, I had expected something a bit more sumptuous than a dingy apartment facing out on a high-street. Bryan fiddled around inside his coat pocket before fetching out his door keys and unlocking the stained door to his apartment, which was up above a flight of narrow stairs completely bathed in darkness. "After you," Bryan smiled, as I walked in ahead of him and clutched onto the handrail while navigating my way through the darkness and up the creaking stairs to his apartment. Arriving at another locked door lit beneath a faded lightbulb, I waited for Bryan to lock the front door to his apartment before he proceeded to walk up the stairs. "So how long have you lived here for?" I asked as the wooden panels of the tapering stairs creaked with each stomping footstep, as Bryan began slowly walking from behind me. "About three years now," replied Bryan, as he crept up from behind me before promptly putting his hands around my waist with my back towards him while facing the locked door. "You're sexy for a Tory," laughed Bryan, as he seductively placed his lips next to my ear while the heat of his lingering breath slowly crept down my neck.

Bryan was seemingly a horny Labour MP who wanted to get me to the polling booth immediately, as he rattled around with his keys before reaching out and unlocking the door. "After you," insisted Bryan again, as I pushed the door open and walked into his apartment.

Walking into a small corridor drenched in total darkness and smelling of mould, I desperately scanned the walls of the room while trying to look for a switch before a quick flick immersed the apartment in bright light. Looking around Bryan's apartment, I wondered if it was better if we were plunged in total darkness, as I observed what could only be best described as a pigsty.

There were empty pizza boxes scattered around the floor with half-eaten crust, while the soiled wallpaper plastered along the walls began to unravel. "Sorry about the mess, I've not had time to clean up properly," gushed Bryan sheepishly, as he locked the door to the apartment.

"Don't worry, it's not that bad," I assured Bryan, while once again willingly lying through the back of my teeth – moving a mucky cup filled with an unknown green substance off the sofa so I could sit down. "Do you want a drink?" offered Bryan, as he proceeded to perch on the sofa to sit down next to me. "No, thank you," I replied, whilst concerned that even touching anything in Bryan's apartment could expose me to some kind of viral outbreak. But before I even had the chance to decontaminate myself, Bryan suddenly put his arm around me. "So, are you going to be my Tory bitch?" whispered Bryan, as he placed his lips close to my quivering ear. I was within proximity of a sexually aroused Labour MP who wanted to have his wicked way with me inside an absolute dump of an apartment in the middle of Tottenham, while not exactly the Ritz, I tried to make the best of a bad situation, as I promptly closed my eyes and placed my lips on Bryan's clenched mouth and proceeded to kiss him.

The slurping sound of our lips locking together filled the vacant quietness of the barren apartment, as I began to feel Bryan's right hand firmly grasp my thigh whilst his other hand continued to caress my neck. "Did they teach you to kiss like that at Eton, Tory boy?" teased Bryan, as his fondling right hand began to creep down from my neck down to my chest at a leisurely pace. "Yes, and they also taught us never to kiss a Labour MP either," I smirked, as I continued kissing Bryan with my eyes firmly closed.

Bryan was, of course, trying to adhere to the stereotype that all Tories were white, upper-class elitists who attended the nursery of England's gentlemen that was Eton College, which was rather ironic considering that new Labour poster boy Tony Blair had also donned the checked trousers and tunic shirts of Eton. Amused, I continued to play up to the warped stereotype of a Conservative Party voter embedded in Bryan's mind and decisively lied that I had attended the hallowed grounds of Eton like Boris Johnson and David Cameron when in reality I had gone to a secondary school which had since been closed down by Ofsted because of failing grades and bad behaviour.

"Shall we go to the bedroom, Tory boy?" suggested Bryan, as I swiftly opened my eyes and pulled my lips back from Bryan's canoodling grip. "Erm... sure," I hesitantly replied, as the prospect of myself and Bryan having sex suddenly dawned on me. Seizing my hand, Bryan stood up from the sofa, while pulling me up from my perched position and lead me to what was seemingly the direction of the bedroom. "I'm going to punish you for the austerity that you have caused, Tory boy," glowered Bryan, as he began to yank on my hand aggressively whilst pulling me into the confines of his bedroom.

Walking over the threshold into his bedroom, Bryan abruptly pulled on my arm and pushed me onto the bed, as I fell onto the squeaky mattress, which fittingly was coloured red. I laid on the king-size bed and looked up startlingly at Bryan, as he stood menacingly at the end of the bed, towering over me as he gazed at me with an intense stare. "Fucking dirty Tory boy," Bryan bellowed, as he hastily started to unbutton his shirt, all while permanently fixated on me.

In the space of a few minutes, Bryan had evolved from a mild-mannered and delicate Labour MP to a crazed psychopath who seemingly wanted to fuck the shit out of me... literally. Still looking up and alarmed at what was happening, Bryan had now fully removed his shirt and thrown it to the floor, as his bare-naked chest stood disrobed, whilst he began to briskly undo the flies on his trousers.

"You're going to be my tank-topped bumboy soon, you Tory bitch!" cautioned Bryan, as he swiftly took off his unzipped jeans and strenuously threw them onto the floor. While calling me a tank-topped bumboy, Bryan had seemingly referred to a 1996 Spectator article in which a younger Boris Johnson had made a humorous remark that had since gone on to furiously enrage homosexual leftists, who had dug up the decade-old article in an attempt to portray the current Prime Minister as some kind of wrathful homophobe.

I giggled as Bryan attempted to use this term to humiliate me as I found it rather humorous and not offensive in the slightest, as he stood towering over me undressed while wearing nothing but his boxer shorts, also fittingly coloured red. "What are you laughing at, you filthy Tory boy?" snapped Bryan, who was seemingly seeing red himself as I giggled at his limp attempt to be menacing. "Sorry, but I can't take seriously a man from the Labour party trying to be masculine," I laughed, as Bryan looked at me with widened pupils and a reddened leer.

I had unintentionally insulted the manhood of a Labour MP and, in doing so, had unleashed a crazed masochist, as the more insults I directed towards Bryan, the more he visibly became aroused. "You far-left anti-Semitic prick!" I yelled at Bryan, as he rapidly pulled down his red coloured boxer shorts, revealing something that almost resembled a fully erected penis. If this was the big Labour Party reveal, then it was truly underwhelming, as what was feebly pointing towards me was something that not even the likes of the IRA or Hamas could boast about.

Still wanting to remain in character as the antagonist Tory, I continued to berate Bryan and his political views, whilst he abruptly grabbed his penis and began masturbating ferociously. "Labour and Jeremy Corbyn are terrorist sympathisers, you make me sick!" I yelled as Bryan's wrist movement became more and more erratic with each passing putdown.

The insults came through thick and thin before Bryan couldn't contain himself any longer, as he swiftly pointed his throbbing penis in my direction. "Suck my dick, Tory boy!" ordered Bryan, as he stood at the end of the bed completely stark naked while intensely tossing off the most microscopic penis that I had ever laid my eyes on.

There was only one way that this political role-play was going to end, and it was with me inserting something that barely measured three inches into my mouth. I felt like Edwina Currie about to go down on former Prime Minister John Major, except instead, I was in a grotty little apartment in Tottenham about to give a blowjob to a Labour MP who got turned on over me lambasting the Labour Party's social housing failure and for dragging the UK kicking and screaming in the Iraq War. "Come on, Tory boy, what are you waiting for?" babbled Bryan, as he held his nether region while twirling it around as if it was some kind of appetising socialist ice cream cone. I took a deep breath and inhaled through my nostrils, as I steadily closed my eyes and crawled towards the end of the bed, where Bryan and his minuscule manhood were waiting.

Reaching the end of the bed and faced with Bryan's penis literally in my face, there was no turning back as I proceeded to open my mouth and push my face forward whilst I began to seductively slurp on Bryan's boner. "Fuck you, Tory boy, you want to privatise the NHS!" moaned Bryan, as he aggressively grabbed the back of my head and mimicked the motion of my head thrusting as I sucked on his penis. Accusing me of wanting to sell the NHS to President Trump aroused Bryan even more, as he forcefully continued to hold onto my head while letting off monstrous sounding groans.

After what seemed like an eternity of performing a blowjob that felt like it was never going to end, it seemed that the grand finale was almost upon us, as Bryan excitedly huffed, "I'm about to erupt!" as I continued to feel the effects of lingering jaw ache. "Fuck... Tory boy!" enthused Bryan, as he tightly grabbed the back of my head, now with both hands intensely trembling – the groans emerging from his mouth becoming increasingly louder with each thrust. "Urgh... Yes... Yes... Yes... FUCK YOU, TORY BOY!" screamed out Bryan... before intensely ejaculating inside my mouth. I had just unintentionally swallowed the semen of someone who was hostile towards Jews and who wanted to take Britain back to the dark ages of the winter of discontent. To say that I wanted to gargle down a tub of holy water at that point was truly an understatement, as Bryan let go of his tightened grip of the back of my head. "Fuck, that was amazing!" announced Bryan, as I sat up from off the bed and made my way towards the bathroom.

I switched on the bathroom light while closing the door from behind me and proceeded to bend my head downwards towards the sink – switching on the tap and guzzling on the flowing water while trying to wash away any lasting remains of socialist semen from the inside of my mouth. While it wasn't the mind-altering adversary sex that I had originally envisioned, at least I could tell my grandchildren that I had sucked off a Labour MP. While not the proudest of achievements that I had accomplished, I nonetheless had no regrets, as I switched off both the tap and light and made my way out of the bathroom.

I quietly tiptoed back into the bedroom, expecting to see Bryan cleaning himself up after the mess he had made, only to be met with the sight of his bare bum sticking out in the air. By ejaculating in the mouth of a Tory, the Labour MP had fallen asleep – laying flat out on his bed while still completely in the nude. "Bryan... Bryan... Are you awake?" I whispered, as I tried to look for any sign of life from the naked Labour MP currently naked and sleeping on his stomach. As the rattling noise of snoring began to vibrate from his sleeping body, I knew that Bryan was well and truly away with the feminist fairies.

Still fully clothed and not wanting to walk the barren streets of Tottenham alone late at night, I perched myself across the edge of the bed and placed my head on the single cushion that was not buried beneath Bryan's stark-naked body. As the deafening noise of intense snoring penetrated my ears, I placed my wearily legs across the bed and yanked the duvet over my body as Bryan slept soundly beside me. If Labour were for the many and not just for the few as they so boldly claimed, then it was in that moment that I realised why I was a Conservative Party voter, as I cosily snuggled up underneath the warm duvet of capitalism, whilst Bryan laid there motionless and cold in the numbing stench of socialism.

CHAPTER 14

ROMANTIC COLLUSION

My vision was murky as I drowsily rubbed my eyes whilst letting out an enormous yawn. I perplexingly scanned around the room as I stretched out my arms and legs simultaneously – letting off a relieving moan as I tried to ponder where exactly I was. It wasn't until I casually looked over to the right side of the bed and saw a stark-naked man vacantly asleep on his stomach that it finally dawned on me where I was and what I had done only a few hours previously.

Bryan was still completely undraped and exposed, as he slept dormant in the same naked position that I remembered him falling into after he had satisfied his kink of being sexually intimate with a Tory. The same thunderous snoring that I miraculously managed to sleep through still ringed from Bryan's sleeping body beside me, as I perched myself up from the bed and performed one final stretch – extending my arms out as far as they could go before letting off another prolonged yawn.

I leisurely walked into the kitchen, still wearing my clothes as I scavenged the cupboards whilst intensely searching for tea bags to make a cup of tea. "Sorry, I'm out of teabags," mumbled a voice, as I hastily turned around to see Bryan standing behind me and still completely in the nude, as I jumped back in startled shock.

While seeing a naked Labour MP would have been enough to give anyone a frightful shock first thing in the morning, the fact that someone who was supposedly English had no teabags in their kitchen was even more traumatising, as I dejectedly closed the cupboard whilst reluctantly accepting that I wouldn't be having a much-needed brew that morning.

"So, what are your plans for today?" asked Bryan, as I awkwardly tried my very best to maintain direct eye contact while not peaking at the shrivelled penis that was just casually hanging there in full view. "Not much," I swiftly replied, as I walked directly past Bryan and back into the bedroom. "Do you want to grab breakfast together maybe?" suggested Bryan, as I proceeded to grab my shoes from off the floor.

While the thought of a scrumptious big breakfast certainty tickled my taste buds, the prospect of casually tucking into a sausage across from a Labour MP who only a few hours prior had ejaculated in my mouth while chastising my political views certainty left a lot to be desired.

"You know what, I'm probably just going to go home," I insisted, as I hastily wiggled my feet into my shoes. I unwillingly found myself in the perplexing of situations after an unfortunate one-night stand in which I just wanted to evade post-haste while embarking on the inevitable walk of shame on the away home. "Well, I'll walk you to the station then," insisted Bryan, whilst standing there still completely in a state of nature.

"No, it's fine, I'll make my own way to the station," I maintained, as the list of excuses in not wanting to prolong this embarrassing situation increasingly dwindled. Just as I thought I would be obliged to have scrambled eggs with someone who wanted to make everyone equally poor and severely reliant on big government under socialism – my phone began to ring.

I fumbled inside my trouser pocket and briskly grabbed my phone to see that Lena was calling me. "Hello," I answered, as I placed the phone close to my ear. "Hey mate, how was your night with the MP?" asked Lena, as Bryan made his way into the bathroom.

Call it divine intervention or just the good luck of the Polish, but Lena phoning me had inadvertently rescued me from having to spend any more unnecessary time with Bryan, as I proceeded to fill her in to over what had happened whilst Bryan remained occupied in the bathroom. "He wants to spend the day with me, but I'm running out of excuses," I confessed, as Lena listened along to the predicament that I found myself in.

"Maybe I could say that I'm meeting you instead?" I proposed as the sound of the toilet being flushed from the bathroom indicated the imminent return of a naked Labour MP. "Sure," laughed Lena, as Bryan plodded out of the bathroom scratching his backside and emphatically yawning. "I'll phone you back in a bit," I told Lena, before hurriedly hanging up, as Bryan woodenly collapsed back onto his bed. "Hey, my friend has just phoned me and reminded me that I had made plans to have breakfast with her this morning," I sighed to Bryan while trying to do my utmost best in looking deprecatory. "Oh, well, that's a shame," sighed Bryan, as his hand steadily ventured down to his exposed nether regions before informingly scratching his bits as if he was engaging in some kind of prehistoric mating ritual. "Well, I guess I'll see you soon," I declared, as I made my way towards the entrance of the apartment. "Maybe we can go out for drinks one night?" urged Bryan, as I fiddled with the lock of the door which had been bolted shut. "Sounds good, I'll let you know," I replied, as I unlocked the door and made my way past the wooden threshold and onto the narrow staircase leading down to the front door to the building. "See you later," I beamed as I closed the door from behind me.

Of course, I was probably never going to see Bryan again, and always wondered why people always professed that they would see somebody later yet had no real intention of seeing them that day at all, or, in my case with Bryan – never seeing them again for the rest of my life. While Bryan was a nice enough person outside of the bedroom, I just didn't envision myself being in a relationship with someone who aggressively scorned my political position each time he climaxed. And while going on the campaign trail with Bryan would surely prove to be adventurous, the thought of canvassing for a far-left socialist Labour Party which had become infested with offensively hostile and abhorrent views towards the Jewish community was just something that I didn't see myself participating in, especially on the day of the Sabbath.

As I made my way down the same creaking stairs that I had trudged up only a few hours prior alongside Bryan, I wondered if I had the energy, or indeed the enthusiasm to walk up a flight of stairs on a date ever again.

According to everyone I had been on a date with within the last month, I was an intolerant bigot and a narrow-minded racist, transphobe and internalised homophobe who would be condemned and cancelled beyond comprehension while wallowing for an eternity in the pits of absolute singleness.

These were dangerous and politically correct times indeed, so dangerous in fact that my dating life had become more high-risk than an Israeli and Palestine blind date.

I was exhausted from the permanently hurt feelings over everything from pronouns to climate change to even muster the strength to swipe right on Tinder, let alone go on another date with another potential social justice warrior or casually exchange semen with a perverted Labour MP as if I was doing a shifty deal with Saudi Arabia in exchange for gold-encrusted dildos. As I made my way down the final step and through the entrance and out onto the street, I took a deep breath and inhaled, whilst making a promise to myself that I wouldn't put myself in such licentious situations again.

I grasped my phone from out of my trouser pocket and gazed at my phone screen as an influx of notifications flashed before my eyes – desperately grasping for my attention in letting me know that the latest batch of emotionally irresponsible, parochially intolerant, and uncongenial misanthropes had eagerly messaged me on Tinder.

It was in that moment as I gazed upon the Tinder app that I had originally downloaded in the hope of finding love that I thought back to all the dates that I had vigorously embarked on within the last month. I went on each date sceptical yet hopeful, but always found myself emotionally deflated by the end of the night. I could feel my thumb motioning towards the privacy option section of Tinder, as I expeditiously swiped down to the bottom of the page before reaching down as far as I could go. And there it was, steadily looking back up at me, as I gazed fixedly at the words… 'Delete Account'.

In that moment of contemplation, I was instantaneously transported back to my fiery date with Ronald, in which he publicly disparaged me for supporting his democratically elected President – shunning me in the middle of Shoreditch before disappearing off into the night. I thought back to the befuddled non-binary Parker who couldn't come to grips with where they were on the gender spectrum, only to settle for a wig and a dress while conforming to one of the two recognised genders a date later.

Then there was Oliver who was living in his very own Spice World – ridiculed and condemned by someone who thought that Geri Halliwell was some kind of philosophical guru. I thought about Harry and wondered if he was still captivated on his phone while murmuring about reducing greenhouse gas emissions to zero. And when it came to Lorenzo, I was just worried whether or not he had made it out of the darkroom alive. And finally, there was Nick, someone who was not a provincial leftist bigot, and someone who did not have malformed body piercings and outlandish blue-dyed hair, and most significantly, someone who I had seemingly formed a connection with, but someone who I had let slip away in a moment of panic, as I distressingly escaped the abyss of the darkroom.

Dating as an openly proud conservative had given me nothing but heartache and gag reflex, and as I reflected upon all the deplorable dates that I had endured with Labour politicians, leftists, Democrats, and gender metamorphosing entities, in one expeditious swipe, I deleted my Tinder account from my phone.

I breathed a huge sigh of relief as I digitally detached myself from the desperate dependency of habitual profiles adorned with conveniently positioned filtered selfies on dating apps, all while standing outside an off-licence on a grimy high-street in the middle of Tottenham. While amid my profound enlightenment, my phone began to vibrate, as I peeked over my phone screen to see that Lena was calling. "Hey, sorry that I didn't phone you back," I apologised to Lena, as I began to make my way across the soiled concrete pavements and towards the direction of the tube station. "That's fine, mate. So, what happened with the politician?" Lena questioned, as I tightly held my phone to my ear while suspiciously scouting the area around me for fear of somebody ready to pounce and mug me. "Oh, well, he blamed me for austerity before ejaculating in my mouth and then falling asleep," I casually replied, as if having the semen of a Labour MP deposited in my mouth was just as ordinary of a transaction as being offered a cup of tea. "That's disgusting!" Lena scolded, as I felt her unequivocal Polish judgement from the other end of the line.

After being indelicately condemned by Lena, we arranged the meeting point to grab breakfast together.

Not wanting to potentially get stabbed as we bit into our hash browns, we both agreed to have breakfast in the more refined surroundings of Covent Garden, as I walked down the feculent smeared steps of Seven Sisters station and onto the Victoria Line. As I perched myself on the same moquette seating that I had flopped on a million times before, I always found it amusing to dissect and analyse the strange and peculiar type of characters that journeyed on the London Underground.

You could always visibly notice the vast contrast of the different type of commuters that tramped onto the carriage as they got off and on their corresponding lines. Men travelling from Highbury and Islington always often had tangled beards that ascended down to their nipples, as the women strutting on the tube were seldom without their aura of superiority and voluminous feminist sloganed t-shirts complete with trademark purple hair and anti-reflection lensed glasses.

For those local commuters travelling past Oxford Circus, they would soon anticipate the arrival of pestilent frenzied tourists, as they rampaged onto the carriage and inflicted absolute disorder and chaos while fiercely holding on to their enormously sized backpacks and suitcases, as travelling Londoners bend their knees inwards like the parting of the red sea. And then, there were those commuters travelling from Brixton, whose physical characteristics were a peculiar hybrid of scruffy tree huggers and tracksuited wearing chavs whose Adidas jogging bottoms were assertively yanked so low that you could grate cheese on their conspicuous bum crack.

I promptly paused my people watching and jumped onto the Piccadilly Line where only a few stops later, I was standing on the bustling cobbled streets of Convent Garden and waiting for Lena to arrive.

"Hey mate," said a familiar-sounding voice, as I felt a faint tap of a hand on the back of my shoulder. I nimbly turned around to see Lena standing there, as she extended out her arms to offer me a hug. "I can't think of someone I would rather see right now!" I gushed to Lena, as I reciprocated with a cuddle of my own. "You've been through hell, haven't you, mate?" teased Lena, as she jokingly referred to my less than stellar dating life. "Tell me about it," I chuckled, as we navigated through the hordes of sightseers mesmerised by the sight of red phone boxes overflowing with calling cards of transsexual prostitutes and Eastern European sex workers, as we made our way to our favourite restaurant to have a full English breakfast.

As we arrived at our table and sat down for breakfast, I meticulously recalled to Lena my night with Bryan and how I had played the role of Tory transgressor in the Labour politician's sadistic fantasy. "Honestly, that sounds seriously fucked up," sneered Lena, as her unceremonious Polish candidness made an appearance just in time for my scrambled egg. "So, when is your next date that doesn't involve any kind of sordid activities?" Lena laughed, as I stirred my tea before delicately tapping my spoon on the side of my cup, just as any etiquette Englishman had become accustomed to doing.

"I'm not too sure," I sighed, as I steadily held my saucer before gently sipping on my tea while affectionally raising my little finger. "I deleted my Tinder account, so I don't think there will be any more dates in the immediate future," I remarked, as Lena continued to judge me with her fixated gaze. "So, what will you do now?" Lena asked, as the waitress firmly placed the bill on our table.

"Focus on my career and maybe do a bit of travelling," I commented, as I hesitantly proceeded to pick up the bill and see what the damage was. "Forty pounds for two English breakfasts and two pots of teas, plus a twelve percent service charge!" I groaned audibly to Lena, as I wallowed in the extraordinary cost of having an English breakfast in London. Maybe I should have stayed in the grotty area of Tottenham and had breakfast in some rundown greasy spoon, I thought to myself, as I reluctantly paid my half for our extortionate breakfast.

We both walked out of the restaurant feeling slightly less financially comfortable than before, as we ambled across to Piccadilly Circus. As we walked across Leicester Square and towards the direction of the Eros statue standing mightily beneath the colourful neon illuminated billboards hanging above the fluttering crowds of people basked in the backdrop of red buses and the faint trickle of raindrops, I couldn't help but notice that everywhere I looked, there were blithesome men and women paired up in twos all around me.

The last time I was here with Lena we had been surrounded by hordes of mincing gay men claiming to be oppressed and victimised while prancing around in little to nothing during gay pride. Now I found myself not being able to walk a few steps without going past a couple who seemingly couldn't keep their hands off each other. It was as if fate was playing a scathing trick on me as we brushed past couples blissfully oblivious and neither aware nor concerned about what was happening around them – gazing vacantly into the eyes of one another as we narrowly tried to avoid them. "Why can't people look where the fuck they're going!" raged Lena, as we evaded enamoured couples homing in around us left, right, and centre.

With the rain beginning to lightly fall beneath us, I thought I had managed to shake off the remaining snippets of overindulgent affection occurring all around us. But as we strolled past the brimming queues spewing out of M&M's World, I immediately felt every wisp of air from my lungs vacate my body.

I stood in the middle of a chaotic street struggling to inhale, to exhale, or do anything, as Lena walked off ahead of me, not noticing that I had abruptly stopped. I tried to call her name to get her to notice me but nothing was coming out of my mouth as I stood there paralysed and breathless. Amongst the busking street performers backflipping for small change and the conceited day-trippers unashamedly snapping selfies halfway on the road with oncoming traffic... there he was.

Someone whom I had formed an extraordinary connection within the most unlikely of places, and most considerably, someone whom I never thought I would see again. As the familiar looking face swiftly walked through the sea of people that had congregated to watch the performing dance troupe whirl and spin, despite the faint drops of rain falling from the greying clouds above them, it felt as if every movement occurring around me had suddenly gone into slow motion.

I stared intensely bewitched and unable to move as he walked closer and closer towards me, and then, within just a heartbeat, he was standing directly facing me.

The astonishment was palpable as the brown-haired figure stood there standing vigorously as if he had miraculously emerged from the darkened shadows and was now basking in the light of day. "Hello, stranger," smiled the familiar face, as I looked on in startled shock. "Hello, Nick," I replied, as a gleeful grin revealed itself from across my face.

Maybe there was a gaping political divide in the country that had destroyed friendships and put an abrupt end to potential romance from flourishing before it even had a chance to prosper and grow, and maybe my dating life had endured a humiliating beating not seen since Labour's excruciating defeat in the 2019 general election, but sometimes, just sometimes, when it comes to love, not even the Russians could rig a relationship that was truly meant to be.

In a modern dating world of leftist censorship and totalitarian ideological conformity, maybe Nick and I would be able to forge a fruitful and extensive relationship without getting triggered and cancelling one another into political oblivion.

Printed in Great Britain
by Amazon